The Vineyard Bride

The Vineyard Sunset Series

Katie Winters

Chapter One

It was the middle of May on Martha's Vineyard, and the island flourished with a wealth of gorgeous flower buds, shimmering green leaves, and frothing waves off the Sound. Soon, tourists would flock to the island, chaotic and loud and eager to take up space all summer long. But just for now, during these blissful weeks, before the season fully began, the Sheridan family was allowed the privacy and quiet of their beautiful home as it dusted itself off from the winter. It was time to live again.

"It's hard to believe we had a blizzard a few months back." Susan Sheridan Frampton stood in a pair of khaki slacks and a white sweater, her hands on her hips as she peered off the back porch of the Sheridan House. Her forehead was tanned from a long afternoon in the garden next door, where she lived with her husband, Scott, and her stepson, Kellan.

Lola Sheridan sat cross-legged on the back patio chair, her head back against the patio furniture pillow and a book splayed open lazily on her lap. Daydreamy and lost

1

inside herself, she couldn't find a way to respond to her older sister.

"And it's hard to believe it's been almost two years since we all came back." Susan continued without waiting for Lola's answer. "And two years since my divorce from Richard!"

"Yes. That tends to happen, doesn't it, Susan? Time passes quickly..." Christine was still just as sharp-witted as ever and quick with sarcastic remarks. She stepped out of the living room with baby Mia strapped to her chest, sleeping.

"What will you do if your daughter inherits your sarcasm?" Susan asked, her smile widening.

"Tell her how proud I am of her," Christine returned. "Sarcasm makes the world go round."

"Really? I heard it was our gravitational pull to the sun," Lola tried.

At this, both Susan and Christine burst into laughter. Just beyond the porch, over the tip-tops of the trees that lined the little forest between the Frampton and Sheridan Houses, a flock of birds crested, forming a strange and beautiful formation in the blue sky. Below them, Grandpa Wes and Kellan stepped out from behind the trees with their binoculars lifted.

"They'll be there all spring and summer long, won't they?" Susan said.

"They'll take breaks for snacks. Don't you worry about that," Christine joked.

Within the house came the sounds of Amanda and Audrey cackling together as they cooked an early dinner.

"That needs more salt and more sugar," Audrey pointed out.

"Audrey. I'm not going to be responsible for making a diabetes dinner," Amanda countered.

"You're absolutely no fun," Audrey shot back.

Lola's eyes connected with Susan's as they shared a laugh. Their daughters, Amanda and Audrey, were mirror images of their mothers and had recently become the best of friends. For Lola, who'd lost touch with Susan for around twenty-five years, this friendship was beyond her wildest dreams. Susan, Christine, and Lola should have been together like this through every decade of their lives.

"What's for dinner, girls?" Susan called as she stepped toward the porch door, which screeched as she opened it.

"We're making chicken burgers," Audrey replied. "With slaw and baked beans and corn."

Lola leaped up from her patio chair, shaking out her overly stiff limbs as she meandered back indoors. Christine followed her, making her way into the Sheridan House just as the screen door closed. On the floor near the couch, Max, now almost fifteen months old, hovered with his hands on the side of the furniture to steady himself.

"There's my baby boy," Lola said sleepily, lifting her grandson against her chest and moving around with him to dance to the music on Audrey's speaker. His little body was so warm, his little hands smooth as silk.

When Lola spun back, she caught Susan's eyes, filled with emotion. Susan's grandchildren still lived in Newark, which was basically a million miles away, and Amanda showed no sign of giving birth anytime soon.

"You want to take him for a twirl?" Lola asked, delivering Max to Susan's outstretched arms.

Max squealed with excitement as Susan danced, her grin widening as their eyes locked.

"Max is such a ladies' man," Audrey said, feigning disdain. "He's going to be a lot to handle when he's a teenager."

"Oh, like you weren't a lot to handle?" Lola teased.

Audrey rolled her eyes at her mother, then began to chop vegetables for a last-minute salad idea. Christine dropped onto the couch, her hand across Mia's head, smoothing the dark hairs. Lola cracked open a bag of chips as Amanda hissed at her, "Don't spoil your dinner."

"I'm not," Lola insisted, crunching on another salt and vinegar chip. "When are the others getting here?"

"The Montgomery clan?" Susan asked. "Andy and Beth said they'd be here around five or so. Charlotte and Claire took the girls to New York this weekend, so they're out. What about Steve, our elusive cousin? Or Kelli?"

"No word on Steve. Kelli's stopping by on her way back from the construction site," Christine informed. "And Aunt Kerry should be here any minute." Kelli and her boyfriend had been hard at work on the redesign of the Aquinnah Cliffside Overlook Hotel.

"No Uncle Trevor, though," Susan affirmed. "Too tired from his procedure yesterday."

The Sheridan women shared a moment of somber silence at the mention of his procedure, which had been a necessary medical checkup but served as yet another reminder that the people they'd always assumed would be around forever might have numbered days.

"They didn't find anything, though," Susan continued. "Healthy as a horse."

"Great news," Audrey chimed in as she sliced

through a green pepper, making the juice splatter across the cutting board.

"Hello? Is anyone home?" A familiar voice rang out from the back entrance near the driveway.

"Is that Cousin Andy?" Lola called, stepping back toward the mudroom. She watched Andy, his pregnant wife, Beth, and her nine-year-old son, Will, as they all removed their shoes and then headed toward the soft light of the living room.

"Will, you're growing like a bean," Lola teased him.

Will stuck out a hand for Lola to shake as Beth explained that Will had recently watched a documentary about business politics and had picked up a few things.

"Business politics?" Lola asked, incredulous.

Will shrugged. "It was on television, and I couldn't find the remote."

"Someone has to rule the world one day. Maybe it'll be you, Will," Beth joked, sliding a hand across her pregnant stomach before she sat on the couch beside Christine.

Will was a darling boy, yet autistic and occasionally difficult to make sense of. Since Andy's romantic relationship with Beth had begun two Christmases back, the Sheridan and Montgomery families had welcomed Will into their folds wholeheartedly, grateful for his idiosyncrasies and his pure outlook.

"And how are you doing, Andy?" Christine asked as Andy limped slightly into the room, proof that his old war injury still had a hold on him.

"Not bad!" Andy returned, his smile enormous. "Still working with the furniture maker."

"I'd love to hire you to make Tommy and I a new bed," Lola began, surprising herself.

"Lola, that's a beautiful idea!" Susan cried.

"You could send me some designs you'd like," Andy affirmed. "I could draw something out for you."

Lola's cheeks burned with embarrassment. What was she thinking, falling in love? Her wedding was in just a few weeks. Was she insane to go through with it, especially now that they'd planned an even more "grand" affair than the failed wedding meant for February?

"Gosh, it's so exciting!" Beth's smile widened to show her adorable cheeks, which had grown the slightest bit since her pregnancy. "Are you planning on having some kind of bachelorette party?"

"No way! I would never plan something like that," Lola returned.

At that moment, a look passed between Audrey and Amanda— one that made Lola suspect that they had a party up their sleeves. Uh-oh. *What are they up to?*

A split second later, boisterous male voices rang out from the driveway, along with two slams of car doors. Amanda nearly dropped her knife as joy played out across her face.

"Is that who I think it is?" Amanda called as the back door opened.

Sam and Noah, Amanda, and Audrey's boyfriends, respectively, stepped through the living room. In their midtwenties, they were suntanned from hours on sailboats, naturally muscular, with ridiculously handsome smiles that took Lola all the way back to her twentysomething dating days (when Audrey had been a little girl).

Amanda rolled up on her toes to kiss Sam on the cheek while Noah wrapped his arms around Audrey, who kept her knife poised over her green pepper.

"Be careful!" Audrey cried, quivering with laughter. "I'm armed, you know."

"Is that a threat?" Noah asked, dropping a kiss over her ear.

"We're filling up!" Susan said, selecting a chip from the bag and placing one on her tongue. "Better have a chip before they're gone."

"With the Montgomery and Sheridan clans around, we'll be eaten out of house and home in no time," Amanda affirmed.

A few minutes later, the rest of the guests arrived— Aunt Kerry and her daughter, Kelli, plus Grandpa Wes, Kellan, Scott, Zach, and, at the very last second, Tommy. Lola's heart seized at the sight of his muscular frame, which was only a shadow as he stepped through the mudroom to join the others. Lola leaped into his arms, inhaling his salty musk from his hours out on the water. Her fingers played out across his muscles and slid down the flat of his stomach. Behind her, the Montgomery and Sheridan clans wandered out toward the back porch, where they could watch the sunlight cascade across the Vineyard Sound.

"I hate to say I missed you today," Lola breathed, just loud enough for only Tommy to hear.

Tommy, who was one-half Italian with olive skin and dark hair, brought his large hands to the small of her back and held her close against him. For a moment, the world stopped moving as Lola closed her eyes, listening only to the laughter of her family members on the back porch and the beating of Tommy's heart.

If Susan hadn't had the courage to come back to the Vineyard two years ago, none of this would have ever happened.

I never would have fallen in love. I never would have become friends with my sisters. I never would have found inner peace.

"Mom. The chicken burgers were ready almost five minutes ago! Are you coming?" Audrey called from the porch. Max, whom she held in her arms, let out a screech of approval.

Lola spun around, linked her fingers with Tommy's, and headed out into the splendor of the springtime evening. Her father sat at the head of the table, gently teasing his sister as he placed baked beans on his plate. Susan and Scott were heavy in conversation about the changes she'd made to their garden. Kellan pointed out that Amanda had a bit of salad dressing on her cheek, which made Sam howl with laughter.

"What happened in there, Amanda? You dunk your head in the salad dressing?" Sam asked, passing her a napkin.

Lola's heart swelled. She and Tommy sat beside one another with their hands still linked beneath the table. Noah poured Lola and Tommy both a glass of wine and chatted to them amicably before turning back toward Max, who jumped around his dinner chair in excitement. Already, Noah was a very dear person in Max's heart.

Will Noah adopt Max one day?

Will Noah become his father?

"I'd like to make a toast," Lola announced, surprising herself.

The rest of the people at the table calmed down, turning their eyes toward the youngest Sheridan daughter. Lola lifted her glass of wine with a quivering hand, catching Susan's eye across the table.

"Susan brought it to our attention that it's been nearly

two years since we all came back," Lola began. "Two years since our lives changed forever. To the current versions of ourselves, this night of chicken burgers and baked beans and funny conversation is just another night. We'll probably do the same thing all over again in a few days, if not tomorrow. But I think it's good to call attention to the fact that we all used to be very, very separate. Back then, Audrey had no idea how to cook anything. And me?" Lola puffed out her cheeks. "I just assumed that people with families they liked were delusional."

"So you're saying we're all delusional, now?" Christine tried, her smile crooked.

"That's exactly right, Chris," Lola said, lifting her glass of wine higher. "To our delusional family. May we always be just this crazy."

The Sheridan and Montgomery members in attendance lifted their glasses joyously, crying out, "Hear, hear," before sipping and falling into another chaotic and beautiful conversation, speaking over one another excitedly.

Beneath the table, Tommy placed a hand over Lola's thigh as he whispered, "You'll be my wife in a few weeks. Nothing could make me happier."

The daydream of springtime had only just begun.

Chapter Two

Amanda's favorite beach on Martha's Vineyard sat along the coastline of the nature reserve Menemsha Hills, on the western edge of the island in Chilmark. Later that week, when the temperature spontaneously jumped up to the midseventies, Amanda headed out of her mother's law offices early and walked straight to the Sunrise Cove to beg Sam to find a way out of work that evening. "Please, Sam. It's the perfect night to watch the sunset..."

Sam's smile was electric. He hustled around the front desk of the Sunrise Cove, the very inn Amanda's grandparents had operated tirelessly, kissed her gently, and whispered, "Didn't I tell you? I don't have to work tonight. I just came in to give Natalie a heads-up about what was happening in room 22."

Amanda's heart leaped into her throat. "What's happening in room 22?"

Sam waved a hand. "The young woman in the room is in a wheelchair, and the wheels keep getting stuck on the rugs around the inn. I had the rugs put in the back room this afternoon to make things easier for her."

The goodness of this man.

"You two have fun tonight!" Natalie called from the doorway that led toward the back office. "Oh, to be young again."

Sam laughed and waved a hand toward Natalie as Amanda tugged him back out onto the front porch of the Sunrise Cove. There, she lifted her chin, closed her eyes, and kissed him with a bursting love, the kind that seemed to take up every square inch of her body and mind and make her float a full inch off the ground. Since she'd first seen him at the Sunrise Cove last year, Sam had never been far from her mind. He'd also proven himself an essential part of the inner mechanisms of the Sunrise Cove Inn itself, thus making everything much, much easier on the Sheridan family as a whole. It couldn't have pleased Amanda more.

"So let me guess. You want to go out to..."

"Menemsha Hills..." Amanda finished his sentence. "Of course."

"You're so predictable, Amanda Harris." Sam curled her dark hair around his finger as a sneaky smile played out across his face. "Luckily, I had a hunch this would happen and already packed up a bottle of rosé and a few other snacks."

Sam had recently purchased a secondhand dark-blue convertible from an older gentleman who lived part-time on the island and frequented the Sunrise Cove Bistro. When seated in the driver's seat with his sunglasses on, Sam looked like the most handsome man on the island (in Amanda's eyes, at least). Beside him in the passenger seat, Amanda dropped her head back as the soft May breeze blew through her curls. The car's speakers howled with an old song from the seventies, which Sam sang along to, nearly getting every word correct.

"You're outrageous," Amanda told him, bubbling with laughter.

"You signed up for this, baby," Sam shot back.

"I really did, didn't I?"

The drive out to Menemsha took about a half hour, stretching south and west toward the Aquinnah Cliffs. Throughout, Amanda and Sam half argued about what to listen to, swapping between the oldies station and the current station, where Amanda's favorite songs played upward of three times an hour.

"If you're going to make us listen to this, then I need you to sing every word," Sam cried, cranking the volume as they sped toward the beach.

"Sam! You know I can't sing."

"Those are the rules, baby."

"Stop calling me baby," Amanda teased, her smile widening.

In truth, she adored being called that. Her ex-fiancé, Chris, had hardly ever used terms of endearment, which had made her feel unwanted and not special in the least. Eventually, Chris left her at the altar in front of all her family and friends, which was much worse than never getting a nickname. To Amanda, it was in the top-ten worst bridal stories she'd ever heard, up there with a friend whose ex-fiancé had left her a month before the wedding for her sister. Well, at least it wasn't that bad.

Sam parked the convertible on the outer edge of the natural reserve, then pressed a button on the roof of the car to bring the top back up.

"Just in case it rains," Sam said as Amanda laughed.

"I've never seen a more beautiful day in my life. There's no way it'll rain."

"We live an island life," Sam countered. "You know that weather can change in the course of five minutes. The only thing we can do is expect the unexpected."

"Wow. Are you a philosopher now?"

"Maybe I am, Amanda. Open yourself up to the secrets of the universe."

Sam leaped out of the convertible and retrieved the tote bag of rosé, plastic cups, and little snacks. Amanda leafed through the back trunk, which was already swirling with chaos despite the fact that he'd had the car for little more than two months, hunting down a picnic blanket.

"Aha." She dragged out the scratchy orange-and-yellow blanket from the back corner, smacking it against the side of the car to get the dust off.

"There's that thing! Looked everywhere for it," Sam cried.

"How the heck do you manage the Sunrise Cove so well?" Amanda shot back.

"I give all my organizational skills to your family's business," Sam returned. "Nothing left for me and my belongings. But you know, a bit of chaos makes things a little more interesting. Don't you agree?"

Amanda's crooked smile drew up toward her left ear. "Do you even know who you're talking to?"

"I know, I know." Sam waved a hand. "This is the woman who makes grocery lists in order of where the items are located in each aisle. This is the woman who made an hourly schedule for what snacks to eat at the Super Bowl Party. This is the woman..."

Amanda leaped up to place a kiss across his lips, ending his tirade. Her heart pounding with longing, she opened her lips against his and closed her eyes. The scratchy blanket caught the wind and flapped against their legs. In the distance, a seagull cawed out ominously.

"This is the woman who loves you," Amanda finished, dropping back down to the sand below.

Sam wrapped his fingers together at the base of her back and held her for a long time, gazing into her eyes. "And this is the man who loves you back."

After a full beat of simmering tension and longing, Amanda stepped back, punched him gently on the upper arm, and teased, "Oh, you're a man now, are you?" before scampering down toward the stone-lined beach. Sam remained hot on her heels, hollering out for her to slow down. But Amanda felt an unwavering sense of energy. She could have run ten miles, even twenty, without slowing down.

She'd never felt this way with Chris. Chris had been a necessary part of her "goal-oriented plans" for her twenties. He'd fit perfectly into the puzzle of "the rest of her life." Sam, on the other hand, had been a blissful surprise, waiting in the wings of her life as she'd fallen into a state of devastation. She'd told Audrey recently, "Sam taught me that you don't always have to have a plan." To this, Audrey had laughed and said, "That drives you crazy, doesn't it?"

Amanda fluttered the orange-and-yellow blanket across a stretch of sand and dropped down to cross her legs and lift her chin toward the orange orb of sunlight as it descended toward the western horizon line. Across the Vineyard Sound and the Atlantic, the next stretch of land was Rhode Island.

"When was the last time you were on the main land?"

Amanda whispered. "It feels like this whole other world. Like I was someone else when I lived over there."

Sam puffed out his cheeks. "It's been since February for me."

"That's right." Amanda remembered that Sam had helped his younger brother, Xavier, move to Providence in February, where he'd begun his first semester at a community college. "Do you miss him?"

"I miss him in a very strange and faraway way," Sam replied contemplatively, splaying his hand across the sand and digging with the tips of his fingers. "He was always getting into so much trouble. That DUI case that your mom helped us with was one in a very long list of problems."

Amanda dropped her head against Sam's shoulder. The water beneath the sun glittered with springtime nostalgia. She could already half imagine missing this night in the near future when they were lost in the throes of summertime bliss.

"Was it hard for you?" Sam whispered then, drawing his hand across her shoulder.

"What?"

"Falling in love again." Sam's words were mere whispers, sweeping across the outer edge of her ear.

Amanda and Sam had never spoken so concretely about their love versus her previous long-term relationship with Chris. Incredibly, Amanda didn't immediately want to change the subject. Instead, she tilted her head and engaged with her emotions. Maybe honesty was better in all cases. Perhaps this was what you needed to do to survive.

"We took it so slow," Amanda whispered, closing her

eyes as a salty breeze flashed across her cheeks. "So slow that I sometimes questioned if you liked me at all."

"You were like a cat," Sam returned sheepishly. "I couldn't get too close to you too quickly. I was terrified you'd run away as fast as you could."

"I really might have."

Amanda's heart swelled, threatening to make her ribs crack. "It all happened the way it was meant to," she added after a long pause. "I truly believe that."

Sam popped the cork from the bottle of rosé and poured them two glasses, which sparkled in bubbling pinks. Amanda's head flashed with images: Chris cracking open a beer before he watched a sporting event on their big-screen TV. Amanda, making list after list of her potential plans for their future— Rutgers University, married by twenty-two, and her first house by twenty-three.

Now that she was twenty-four, there could be no more lists. No more dreaming. Not even: Sam Fuller, carrying an infant child across his chest.

Whatever will be, will be.

Sam crunched on a chocolate-covered peanut and passed her the bag. Amanda allowed the morsels to melt across her tongue, watching as the waves frothed across the sands. A little girl far down the beach tossed stone after stone into the water as though she wanted to prove something. *Imagine us coming here with our children. Imagine us, here together for the next fifty years.*

"I guess I should just tell you how happy I am," Amanda whispered. "I don't know if I've ever been this happy before. And sometimes, it terrifies me. I've lost so much. I've watched my parents get divorced. I've watched Audrey have the baby of a man who wanted nothing to do with her. I've watched my ex-fiancé run all the way across the world, as far away from me as he could get."

Sam set his jaw, his eyes catching the last light from the glittering sun. "Do you feel like you can trust me, Amanda?"

Amanda swallowed the lump in her throat. With her eyes locked on his, she whispered, "Yes. I think I can trust you. Do you feel like you can trust me?"

"More than anyone."

When the last of the sunlight diminished westward, headed across the great continent of North America, Sam and Amanda gathered their half bottle of wine, empty packaging, and blanket and headed back to Sam's convertible.

"I told you it wouldn't rain," Amanda teased as she folded up the blanket and placed it gently in the trunk.

"You think you're a meteorologist, huh?"

Amanda laughed as she danced around the side of the car and dropped into the passenger seat. As she settled in, buckling her seat belt, her eyelids fluttered closed, and her shoulders dropped back. She felt languid and sleepy, as though she was a little girl about to be carried into the house by Richard Harris, her father.

"Where are we headed?" Sam asked gently as he started the engine. "The Sheridan House?"

"That sounds good," Amanda breathed.

"Just close your eyes," Sam murmured, drawing a hand over her knee as he eased the car out of the beach parking lot. "We'll be home in thirty minutes."

"No. I should stay awake. Keep you company."

"Don't worry about me." Sam laughed. "I got my oldies station on. I'll be all right."

"You're such an old soul," Amanda murmured, her eyelashes drifting across her cheeks.

During those blissful and dark moments of sleep, Amanda's mind took her into a sort of abyss of dreams— chasing Audrey through the hills of Martha's Vineyard; lacing a sailing rope through her fingers as she and Sam sped out across the Sound; listening to the laughter of Grandpa Wes and Kellan as they watched a bird from the window.

This is real life.

If you don't stop to look around for a moment.

You'll miss it.

The sudden bright flash of light erupted over Amanda's face. Next came a terrifying honk and the sound of shattering glass. As Sam smashed his foot against the brake and cried out, Amanda was yanked forward, caught painfully with the seat belt. Glass wavered across her fingers and her thighs. She blinked through the terrifying light of the vehicles, trying to make sense of what was before her.

Glass. Bent metal. The smell of burning oil.

"Sam!? Sam!?" Amanda heard herself scream her boyfriend's name with pure terror. "Sam, are you all right?"

Have I lost my love all over again?

Chapter Three

What happened next shocked Amanda to her core. Quivering, she stretched her arms out to investigate the shards of glass that had struck her. Little flecks of blood oozed out across her porcelain skin. She then turned her face to the left to watch as Sam unbuckled his seat belt and called out to her, his eyes wide.

"Amanda! Do you hear me? Amanda, are you all right?"

Lost in the nightmare of these strange moments, Amanda felt herself nod. Sam then rammed into the driver's door with his shoulder and jumped into the darkness outside. "I need to check on the others!" he called back to her.

As delicately as possible, Amanda flicked the glass from her arms and stepped from the car. A long string of blood oozed down her arm and stained her dress.

Once outside the car, she tried to make sense of what had happened. A maroon Chevy Cavalier had pulled out from a dark road directly in front of an approaching BMW. The maroon Chevy and the BMW had practically knocked heads, casting billowing smoke into the night's air. The accident had happened so swiftly that Sam, coming up the hill behind the BMW, hadn't had time to stop and smashed into the tail end of the BMW, crunching both his front and their back.

In the shock that hung in the air immediately after the crash, Sam hobbled toward the BMW, which looked worse for wear. Every second seemed to stretch on for at least a minute, making it difficult to understand when, exactly, the crash had occurred. Their lights remained on, casting a ghoulish glow between the trees on that back country road.

"Sam?" Amanda cried, suddenly terrified. She wanted to wrap her bloodstained arms around him and hold him close. She wanted to call Susan to pick them up and take them back home.

"Stay back, Amanda. There's broken glass everywhere," Sam called.

At that moment, the Chevy Cavalier that had slammed into the front of the BMW turned its engine on. Amanda stayed back, genuinely shocked as the Chevy unlatched itself from the BMW. The driver drove its hind end down the road it had come out from, performing a wheel-screaming U-turn and casting itself back into the darkness. The vehicle was gone in an instant, leaving the two cars behind.

"What the hell!" Sam called out, his voice echoing out across the woods. Amanda had never heard him filled with such rage.

Unable to hold herself back any longer, Amanda

hustled around the back of the convertible and wrapped her arms around Sam. He remained frozen in surprise, with a gash and blood across his forehead that made him look like an action star.

"I can't believe this!" Sam muttered, aghast. "They just drove away after causing this accident." He then snapped his fingers and leafed through his pocket to grab his phone. "DTXQ12. DTXQ12."

"Sam? What are you talking about?"

"The license plate," Sam shot back. "I caught a glance when the jerk made a U-turn."

Sam's fingers flashed over the screen of his phone as he noted the license plate. As he finished, a wail came out from the BMW. Amanda moved forward as quickly as she could, although her legs quivered with panic with each step.

"Sam! Call 911!" she screamed back as she approached the BMW to discover an older woman in her sixties, her head sloped back against the seat rest and a bloody hand across the steering wheel. The shattered windshield cast glass across the woman's thighs and arms. Her closed eyelids caught the strange light from her headlights, which bounced back from the trees.

"Oh my God," Amanda whispered, pressing her palms together as she leaned down to speak to the older woman. "Can you hear me?"

The woman moaned in response.

"Ma'am, please don't move around at all. You're covered in glass," Amanda coaxed. "We have an ambulance coming. You'll be taken care of. I promise you that."

Amanda remained stationed at the front of the BMW, eyeing the damage from the corner of her eye. Black tire tracks led from the main road out into the woods, proof that the guy had wanted to get out of there fast.

Behind her, Sam called 911, describing where they were on State Road, near the North Tisbury Farm, about halfway between the beach and the Sheridan House. "There was a hit-and-run," Sam explained. "The guy just hightailed it out of here, but I managed to write down the license plate number."

"What kind of person would do this?" Amanda asked Sam as he hung up and joined her at the front of the BMW.

"I don't know. I've never seen anything like it."

Behind them, the woman no longer moaned with any sign of injury. Instead, she remained silent, which was so much worse.

"I'll call Mom," Amanda whispered, her hand trembling as she brought the phone to her ear. The call rang out across the night before finally reaching the cozy ecosystem of Susan and Scott's cabin along the water.

"Honey! How are you? You snuck out of the office today."

"Mom. Don't freak out." Amanda's voice was strained as she described all she could about the past five minutes. Throughout, Susan was quiet yet clearly terrified.

"Sit tight, honey. I'll come to pick you and Sam up right this minute. Does Sam have an emergency kit in the trunk? Maybe station some flares, so other vehicles can see you."

Amanda and Susan, both ultra-prepared for something like this, always kept an emergency kit in the trunk. "I'll check," Amanda muttered, cursing herself for her lack of preparation. She had a hunch (soon verified) that Sam wasn't as prepared as she would have been.

"Get out of the road," Susan ordered. There was the jangle of her keys and the rush of her spring jacket over her shoulders. After a split second, during which she muttered something off the phone to Scott, Susan added, "Honey? I love you. I love you to bits. I'll be there soon."

About ten minutes later, they heard the first of the sirens. They roared out across the wooded hills, screeching against the somber serenity. Red lights flashed across the surrounding trees as the ambulance and two police vehicles arrived and made a perimeter. Amanda and Sam pulled back, watching as the EMT worked diligently, opening the car door delicately and taking scissors to the woman's seat belt.

Two cops approached Sam and Amanda and asked them a series of initial questions. Sam took the reins, describing the crash. When they asked Amanda what she'd seen, she said, "I was fast asleep until the crash. After that, all I saw was that monster driving away from the scene as fast as he could."

"Or she," Sam reminded them. "We couldn't see the driver at all. But I have the license plate." He leafed again through his pocket to draw out his phone to translate the number to the officers.

"Amanda!" Susan's voice rang out across the scene of the accident. She'd parked about twenty feet to the north of the police vehicles and ambulance and waved both arms wildly like a flight coordinator. Scott stood beside her with a hand raised over his eyes to peer through the flashing lights.

As Sam continued to speak to the authorities, Amanda hustled around the ambulance and flung into her mother's arms. Susan Sheridan was everything she'd always been— warm, smelling of lavender and whatever she'd cooked for dinner that night, ready with an encouraging word and a hand to smooth over her hair.

"It's okay, honey. You're okay." Susan repeated this like a song, wrapping her arms around Amanda and shifting left, then right.

A few minutes later, the EMT managed to lift the stretcher into the back of the ambulance. The doors pounded closed behind the stretcher, and the vehicle again let out that horrible shriek. Susan, Amanda, and Scott hustled out of the way and watched as the ambulance rushed back to the Oak Bluffs hospital. Amanda said a tender, silent prayer for the woman on the stretcher — a woman out for a drive in the darkness, headed for a terrible fate.

Sam finished with the police officers and headed toward Susan, Scott, and Amanda. The blood on his face had dried and now looked like Halloween makeup. Amanda shifted from Susan to Sam and burrowed her head against his chest, listening to the whack-whack of his heart. *We're alive. We're okay,* she told herself. *We got through this together.*

"I can't wait till they find the person who did this," Sam muttered angrily, his eyes cast back toward the two crunched-up vehicles.

It took some coaxing, but Susan finally dragged Sam back to Scott's truck. Once there, Sam and Amanda slipped into the back seat and buckled themselves up, their fingers latched tightly together. Amanda had to fight the urge not to beg Scott to drive ten miles an hour. Sam spent most of the drive back to the Sheridan House with his chin to his chest.

"Everyone's back at the house waiting for you," Susan said from the front seat. "Christine's already making a big pot of clam chowder. Audrey says she's cracked your favorite bottle of wine."

"God, how I love my family." Amanda couldn't muster the strength to laugh much at all. When she looked down at her hands, they still shook uncontrollably.

When Scott parked out back, Audrey, Lola, and Christine hustled out of the Sheridan House, their eyes marred with concern. Amanda and Sam eased out of the truck, already stiff from the accident. A blotchy-faced Audrey rushed toward Amanda and hugged her gingerly, which was such a role reversal. Normally, Amanda felt like she had to handle Audrey with care.

"Thank God you're in one piece. What happened?" Audrey asked, breathless.

Amanda shook her head. "I heard you cracked that bottle of wine."

Audrey nodded knowingly and guided Amanda into the Sheridan House, past a bug-eyed and fearful Christine and Lola. Sam stepped in after her, his hand cupping her elbow. Amanda sensed that they couldn't be far away from one another, not that night. Not after what they'd been through.

A big pot of clam chowder bubbled on the stovetop. Max bobbed around on the floor at Grandpa Wes's feet, smacking his palms together.

"He won't sleep," Audrey grumbled. "I think he knew you were coming back." She dropped down to draw Max into her arms, where he bobbed excitedly, greeting Amanda.

Christine poured Sam and Amanda glasses of wine; her brow furrowed knowingly. Christine understood that you didn't always want to talk about your pain. Grandpa Wes's eyes were wounded, yet he kept silent, as well. Lola hurried to the speaker system and put on a Jim Croce album, which brought a collective sigh of relief.

"We're just glad you're okay," Susan finally added. There wasn't anything else to say.

Exhausted, Amanda and Sam stepped into the bedroom that Amanda had taken as her own, there downstairs next to Grandpa Wes's in the add-on that Scott had built over a year ago. With the door closed behind them, Amanda and Sam curled up on Amanda's mattress and stared at the new white walls. Outside, there was the murmur of the rest of the Sheridan clan. It wasn't difficult to imagine their current topic of conversation. Amanda was just grateful she couldn't make out their specific words.

"Please, don't go home tonight," Amanda breathed into Sam's chest.

"There's no way you could get me to leave," Sam murmured back, his hand stretching across the back of her head.

"Really?"

"I told you, baby. I'm in this for the long haul." Sam's eyes watered longingly before he closed them and kissed her gently.

The long haul.

"Don't they always say, 'In sickness and in health?' And what's the other one... 'From car accident to car accident?'"

"I think that's the expression," Amanda affirmed with a soft laugh.

"Good."

Did this mean Sam wanted to propose to her?

"I love you, Sam," Amanda whispered, her voice

hardly anything at all as she drifted off to sleep. "Thank you for taking care of us today."

By the time Sam answered her, Amanda had drifted off to the land of dreams once more. But they remained like that all night long, tucked safely against one another, grateful for the time they had left.

Chapter Four

Lola drove bleary-eyed back to the cabin in the woods she shared with her fiancé, Tommy. In the driver's seat, she sat in the darkness of the driveway, watching as Tommy's shadow eased from one end of the cabin to the other, preparing for bed. Through one curtain, she watched his shadow as he rinsed off the bowl he'd used for dinner. In the next panel, he stood before the television for another minute, catching the last moments of whatever show was on. Then he disappeared into the back of the house to brush his teeth and splash water on his rugged and handsome face. Lola's heart pattered wildly, the way it often did when she felt endlessly grateful for what she had.

That was the thing about accidents. When other people experienced potential loss, Lola swam in their trauma, terrified that something like that could eventually come for her and Tommy and Audrey. If she'd had to pick Audrey up from an accident site, she would have sobbed through the whole thing. Susan was so much stronger than she was. That, or maybe she was just better at pretending she was strong enough to go on. That seemed like the Susan Sheridan way.

Once inside the cabin, Lola removed her spring jacket and hung it on the coatrack nearest the door. Her shoes off, she walked softly through the kitchen and the back hallway, charting the course back to where Tommy remained on the other side of the bathroom door. There came the sound of his swishing his mouth clean with mouthwash, then the rush of the water as he cleaned out the sink. When he opened the door to find Lola, he nearly leaped back with fear.

"Lola!" His eyes widened. "I thought you were staying at the Sheridan House tonight."

"I just had to come back to see you," Lola murmured, genuinely lost in the sea of her own fears. She stepped into his burly arms and pressed her cheek against his chest as her legs shivered beneath her. *I never want to lose you, Tommy. Never, ever.*

Together, Tommy and Lola sat at the kitchen table over mugs of steaming tea and watched the dense night outside the window. Lola explained what she knew of the accident and that she couldn't calm the quaking fears in her mind, which forced her to come up with horrible conclusions about her own future.

"You're safe," Tommy whispered finally, a hand wrapped around hers. "We're all safe. We're going to be all right."

Not long after that, Tommy's cell rang out across the house. Tommy cursed himself for not putting it on silent and then cursed technology. "We don't need these stupid devices."

Lola stepped toward the sink to clear out the mugs of tea, listening as Tommy answered. The clock on the wall read 11:47 p.m. Who could be calling at that hour?

Tommy reappeared in the kitchen, his face blotchy. "Yeah? My number? I don't understand..."

Lola bristled at the confusing one-sided conversation. She whirled around, one mug still lifted, to watch as Tommy collapsed at the kitchen table.

"You're kidding." Tommy shook his head and dropped his forehead onto his palm. "Beatrice. Wow. I had no idea she was even on the island."

Lola dropped the mug into the sink with a thwack and joined Tommy at the kitchen table, her eyes heavy with fear. Who was Beatrice? Tommy's face illustrated confusion, sorrow, and something else— something primal that she couldn't fully name.

"What happened?" Tommy demanded then, which forced Lola to listen to the in-between silence, during which she could only guess what the other person on the line explained.

"I'd love to come up tonight," Tommy muttered.

Lola's heart skipped three beats. *Up where?* No ferries ran this late at night, which meant that whatever this was, it was on the island.

"Okay. Thank you. Thank you for everything," Tommy sighed into the phone. "Good night." He then shuddered as he lay the phone back on the table and placed his fingers over his cheeks.

"Tommy. Talk to me," Lola whispered, terrified of whatever came next.

"My great-aunt Beatrice," Tommy muttered. "She's up at the hospital tonight after a car accident."

Lola's eyes widened. *A car accident?* She slightly remembered what Amanda had said about the other driver involved in the hit-and-run, an older woman in her sixties who'd hardly been conscious in the moments after the crash.

"Your great-aunt Beatrice?" Lola balked, remembering the name from Tommy's list of people he wanted to invite to the wedding. "I had no idea she was on the island."

"Me neither. Apparently, they found my number on a sheet of paper inside the purse they brought back from the accident. Since she's a senior, she wasn't so keen on things like..." He lifted his cell phone, acknowledging the technology he'd only just cursed a few minutes ago. "Anyway. Aunt Beatrice doesn't have much family to speak of besides me, which is why they used that phone number. It was their only way forward."

"Did they say how she is?" Lola whispered.

"She was unconscious for a good two hours when they admitted her after the accident, but they were recently able to talk with her about simple things, like the weather and the date. I asked about coming up tonight, but they said it was better to wait until the morning." He shivered, disgruntled. "I have no idea why she's here so many weeks before the wedding. And no idea what to do next."

"All we can do is offer our support," Lola whispered, stepping up to drop herself onto Tommy's lap and kiss him delicately on the cheek. "We'll be at the hospital first thing tomorrow morning and comfort her all we can."

"I hardly know the poor woman," Tommy murmured. "She's the last link to my mother."

Tommy's mother had passed away earlier that year, an event that had rocked him to the core in ways that had surprised Lola. Prior to his mother's death, Tommy had

31

seemed the kind of guy who didn't uphold the power of family. Now, with a wedding on the way, a true love for his ex-stepdad, Stan, and a wealth of relationships with the rest of the Sheridan clan, that couldn't have been further from the truth.

Before Lola led Tommy to bed that night, Tommy made sure his shift was cleared on the freight line the following morning. Over the winter and springtime, he'd taken over multiple shifts for Scott Frampton's freight liner, often waking up before four in the morning and returning by noon. As summer approached, Tommy's work on the freight liner had grown increasingly infre- quent— especially as he'd taken up work at the sailing docks once more, a space he called "where his heart belonged."

"We'll be up there by visiting hours," Lola whispered to him as they fell into a deep sleep, her hand stretched across the coarse hairs of his chest.

But the final thoughts her mind gave her before unconsciousness were *I knew we weren't safe. I knew something was wrong.*

She couldn't shake this eerie feeling, not even in dreamland, where nightmares shrouded her mind.

* * *

Hospital visiting hours began at ten o'clock the following morning. Heavy with anxiety, Lola and Tommy idled in Tommy's truck outside the hospital at nine thirty as the radio spat between stations, unable to hold the tune.

Lola had already reported the news of the potential hit-and-run victim's identity as Tommy's Great-Aunt Beatrice to her sisters, daughter, and niece. The Sheridan women group chat was a live wire that morning, kicking out words of encouragement, empathy, and confusion all at once.

> SUSAN: The poor woman.

> CHRISTINE: What was she doing on the island so soon? Your wedding's not for another few weeks...

> AMANDA: I feel terrible that this happened.

> AUDREY: Tell us everything when you meet her!

At ten on the dot, Tommy and Lola reported at the front desk of the hospital and followed a nurse in light-blue scrubs to Aunt Beatrice's room, where she'd been moved after the severity of her injuries had dissipated. Lola and Tommy remained wordless until they stood in the doorway, peering down at a very tiny woman with wrists the size of a child's and dyed blond hair that curled wildly around her ears and across her shoulders. Gashes from the glass covered her cheeks and arms, and she wore a significant bandage across her upper arm, proof that something in the accident had gotten her good.

Two bright-blue eyes peered out from the propped-up pillow. After a moment of quiet surprise, Beatrice called out, "Tommy! Is that really you?"

Tommy leaped for the seat at her bedside, drawing both hands forward to take her tender one in his. "Aunt Beatrice." He staggered through his words, incapable of making much sense. "What are you, I mean. What are you doing here?"

Beatrice's smile was secretive and genuine, the sort of thing she didn't show everyone. "I came for your wedding, of course."

"But Aunt Beatrice, the wedding isn't for another few weeks," Tommy protested.

Beatrice cast her eyes to the glittering white sheets. For a split second, Lola thought that maybe the woman was losing her mind. Maybe she'd lost track of the date of the wedding. Perhaps the loss of Tommy's mother, her niece, had devastated her so much that she'd lost her memories, which was what had happened to Lola's Aunt Willa.

"It's terribly embarrassing," Beatrice began tentatively.

"You can tell us anything," Lola offered. "We're family."

Beatrice nodded contemplatively, placing her white teeth across her lower lip. "I've given my life to my naturopathy practice up in Boston. A few months ago, I parted ways with my longtime partner and closed the practice. In the wake of that closure, I haven't quite known what to do with myself. So I applied to work as a naturopathy doctor at the Katama Lodge here on Martha's Vineyard. I'm so excited at the prospect of living out my last few decades just a little ways away from the both of you."

Lola, who adored the Katama Lodge and Wellness Spa and the very kind Remington-Grimson-Potter women who worked there, pressed a hand over her heart at the idea.

"I didn't want to tell you that I had this interview," Beatrice continued sheepishly. "I have this idea that if you say what you want too loudly to other people, you'll curse yourself, and it won't come true. I guess I'm a tad superstitious."

"Oh, Aunt Beatrice. You would be fantastic at the Katama Lodge." Tommy's voice was tender, like an adoring father.

"Yes, well. The interview is slated for tomorrow!" Beatrice explained. "I don't suppose I'm in any shape to go talk to Janine Grimson about my current health beliefs. Not with a million slashes across my arms and legs."

Lola bristled, surprised again at the contrast between this woman's injuries and the brightness of her personality.

"What happened exactly?" Lola asked.

"Gosh, I don't know. The accident is a blur for me," Beatrice continued. "I remember I was driving out on State Road. And after that, it's a blank." She snapped her fingers to illustrate how quickly it had gone.

"We're pretty sure that my niece and her boyfriend were involved in the crash, as well," Lola explained timidly. "And they reported that the person responsible for the accident drove away from the scene of the crash."

Beatrice's lips formed a round O. She eyed Tommy, incredulous, as her fourth finger twitched against her leg. "Some people just don't know how to live in the world, do they?"

Tommy shook his head and dropped his eyes to the ground as though he was too heavy with guilt to deal with it.

"Well, whatever it is they're going through right now, I wouldn't wish it on my worst enemy," Beatrice sounded after that. "The guilt of running away from an accident! Can you imagine?"

Lola couldn't help but smile. What a surprising thing

to say; what a beautiful perspective. Beatrice deserved to be back out in the world, ready to pass on the intricate details of her naturopathy degree and to heal the souls of Martha's Vineyard, one guest after another. As soon as she got out of that bed, that is.

Chapter Five

Lola and Tommy spent the better part of the morning and afternoon in that sun-kissed hospital room, digging into conversation with the wise and beautiful Beatrice and finding new ways to cope in the wake of the horrible thing this stranger had done. Mid-afternoon, Tommy admitted that he had to head down to the docks to meet with several sailing students, which pushed Beatrice to confess she was terribly exhausted and needed a few hours to rest.

"I'm sure they won't keep me here much longer," she added.

"Oh! Before we go, we should call the Katama Lodge and explain that you need a bit more time before the interview," Lola cried, drawing her phone from her pocket.

"Let me, honey." Beatrice ruffled through her purse to find her address book, an old-fashioned thing, then grabbed the phone by the bedside table to call the Katama Lodge and Wellness Spa. The sharp gashes on her arm caught the sunlight and played in contrast to how sure of herself she sounded on the phone. "Hello. Good afternoon, Mallory. My name is Beatrice Cunningham. Curious if I could speak to Janine Grimson? Thank you."

Tommy and Lola waited with bated breath as Beatrice explained the dynamics of her current situation and explained she could "probably" come into the Lodge the following week sometime, as she planned to be on the island for the better part of the month for her great-nephew's wedding. "That's right. Tommy Gasbarro! You know him?" Beatrice's eyes glittered as she continued to converse with Janine. "He is quite handsome, isn't he? He and Lola make the perfect pair."

When Beatrice got off the phone, she placed it delicately back in its bedside cradle, lifted her chin, and said, "That's settled. Janine passes on her regards. Apparently, the two of you are quite famous here on the island. Tommy, you always said you didn't want anything to do with people or building a community. What happened?"

Tommy's laughter was uproarious. He drew his arm across Lola's shoulders and draped her against him. "You know what I've learned since spending more time in one place, Aunt B? People can change."

"They certainly can," Beatrice affirmed, snapping a finger against the small point of her nose. "You kids run out there, now. Leave this old woman in peace."

* * *

Tommy dropped Lola off at the Sunrise Cove Inn before he headed for the Edgartown docks, where Tommy planned to teach sailing lessons. Lola kissed him adoringly, her eyes closed, then leaned back to gaze at his tanned face and broad shoulders. She couldn't tell him over and over again how handsome he was, could she? It was too much.

"I'm just so glad she's okay," Lola breathed.

"Me too." Tommy shook his head delicately. "I can't believe she never mentioned she was coming into town early."

"She sounds like she's on the brink of building a brand-new life," Lola countered. "She probably didn't want anyone's advice yet."

"And now, she's locked away in a hospital bed."

"That isn't her fault."

"Didn't you say Sam saw the license plate?" Tommy asked.

"He sure did, and he gave it to the police," Lola told him. "I wonder what's going on with that."

"Check, will you?"

Lola agreed. She then stretched herself over the middle of the truck and kissed him a final time before whispering, "I swear to God, Tommy, you'd better drive safe."

Lola slid out of the truck and headed for the front desk of the Sunrise Cove. The walk from the street in front of it, through that glorious old-fashioned front door, was a walk she'd performed upward of a million times. If she gave herself permission for a split second, she could imagine that Anna Sheridan, her mother, would appear at the front desk, ready with a big platter of cookies or a hug.

Instead, Sam and Amanda peered back from the other side of the desk. Their enormous eyes proved they were still shell-shocked from the accident the night before.

"How are you holding up, you two?" Lola asked

tenderly, dropping her elbows on the front desk.

"It's good to be here. It keeps our minds off everything," Amanda returned. "How is Aunt Beatrice? I can't believe she was that woman in the other car." Her eyes became stormy, dipping back into the memories from the previous night.

"She's doing just fine," Lola returned. "I'd never met her before, but she seems like a spitfire if I ever met one. She's in her sixties, but her mind is sharp as a tack."

Amanda's smile widened.

"Does she remember the accident?" Sam asked.

"No. Nothing at all," Lola affirmed. "Which is probably for the best."

"Yeah. It's still weird to have lost this huge chunk of time, though," Sam countered.

"Mom!" Audrey appeared in the hallway between the Sunrise Cove Bistro and the Sunrise Cove Inn itself, carrying little Max in her arms and jumping around excitedly. "I didn't know you were stopping by."

Lola stretched her arms out to little Max, cradling the toddler against her as he buzzed his lips.

"You've been at the hospital all this time?" Audrey asked, her hand wrapped tenderly around Max's right foot.

"Yes. Aunt Beatrice is doing all right. But seeing her like that, all banged up, has me even angrier than I was before." Lola swallowed the lump in her throat and then asked, "Sam, you said you gave the license plate number to the police. Have you checked up on that?"

"Not yet," Sam told her. "I don't want to pressure them."

Lola's laughter was dark and gritty. "I've been a journalist for more than twenty years. I know how to put pressure on people to get the information I need."

"You sound terrifying, Mom," Audrey shot back.

"Audrey. You're a budding journalist in your own right. You know exactly what I mean."

Audrey nodded, her smile fading. "I know."

A little while later, Christine appeared at the Sunrise Cove carrying a little Mia across her chest. Zach hustled out from the Bistro kitchen to greet his baby and lifted a hand to the other Sheridan crew. His cheeks were blotchy from the heat of the kitchen.

At their corner table, Lola sipped a glass of Riesling and tilted her head, watching the ease with which Christine and Zach now conversed with one another. Zach's hand-stretched across Mia's head as his thumb traced the dark strands of her hair. *Could Tommy and I ever...*

But no. Audrey was the only daughter she'd ever needed. If she and Tommy had a child (not that they'd discussed it in any concrete way), their lives would shift forever— and not always in the best of ways. The Tommy Gasbarro she knew and loved could sail off to glorious Caribbean islands at a moment's notice. With Lola becoming a Gasbarro herself, she had a right to a seat on that sailboat. She had a right to the adventurous world of Tommy's life.

But a baby of their own. Tommy as a father. Audrey's father had taken off just as soon as he'd gotten enough money. They hadn't heard from him much at all since Audrey had been a toddler. Good riddance.

"Where'd you go?" Audrey asked, snapping a finger in the air to yank her mother back to reality.

Lola forced a smile and refocused her attention. Amanda, seated to the left of Audrey, had her fists against her cheeks and glared down at her untouched glass of wine.

"Amanda," Lola began tentatively, drawing her hand across Amanda's elbow.

Amanda jumped slightly, her large eyes proof that she'd been somewhere far away.

"Why don't I call the police, now? See what's up with the license plate?"

"That would be fantastic," Amanda breathed.

Lola nodded, drawing her cell from her purse and dialing the local police station. The front desk secretary greeted her primly, sounding over-important.

"Hello, Oak Bluffs Police Station. This is Connie speaking."

"Hi, Connie. I wondered if you could help me out with something. My niece was involved in a hit-and-run accident last night on State Road. Her boyfriend, one of the drivers, was able to give the license plate number of the vehicle that left the scene to the officers. We're curious if anything came of that."

"Came of what?"

Lola rolled her eyes into the back of her head. Was this woman dense, or what? "Curious if the police were able to locate the owner of the vehicle. A Chevy Cavalier, I believe."

Amanda nodded furiously.

Connie chewed gum into the phone speaker. "I don't believe you're at liberty to ask such a question."

Lola's cheeks burned red with anger. "I'm a prominent journalist across New England. I believe it's standard to release such information to the public. If it's not common practice at your station, I'd be happy to write an article on the subject."

Connie muttered something Lola couldn't fully understand before hollering back into the belly of the station about "some woman who wanted information on the hit-and-run case."

As she'd half expected, Lola knew the cop in charge of the case itself. She'd gone to school with Freddie at Oak Bluffs High more than twenty years ago.

"Freddie! It's been ages. How's your family?" Lola began joyously, taking over the conversation the way she'd learned to back in her early journalist days.

"Lola Sheridan. It's been, what, six months? I heard about your new claim to fame as director of Martha's Vineyard plays and musicals."

"Just the one musical so far, Freddie. I think my thespian days are through."

"Sad to hear." Freddie's voice bounced around. He was clearly happy to hear from her. "Connie said something about the hit-and-run case from last night?"

"Yes. My niece was involved, and her boyfriend managed to pass along the license plate information. Have you been able to track that plate?"

Freddie heaved a sigh into the speaker. Lola furrowed her brow. This didn't sound good.

"We did, yes," Freddie continued. "First thing this morning. Unfortunately, that particular Chevy Cavalier was reported as stolen from a Boston area family a little more than a week ago."

"Stolen." Lola's heartbeat pumped in her ears. "No wonder they drove away quickly."

"We thought the same. It's not the sort of thing a typical islander would do, that's for sure. Now we have the task of watching hours and hours of CCTV footage from the ferries between Woods Hole and Oak Bluffs, trying to find the vehicle involved."

"Good idea," Lola said.

"But the angle of the camera is a bit strange. And the vehicle count is, of course, in the thousands. It'll be easy to miss," Freddie told her. "On the one hand, we're on an island, which means that it should be easier to track down whoever did this. On the other hand, if someone wants to stay hidden, we can't very easily drag them out of nowhere."

"I hear you, Fred." Lola dropped her gaze to her newly painted fingernails, which flashed deep red in the sunlight. "Keep me updated if anything changes."

"Sure will."

Lola returned her cell to her purse and blinked back up to Amanda, whose face was scrunched up like a pug's.

"Doesn't sound good," Amanda tried.

"Whoever caused this accident isn't exactly winning any awards in community service," Lola returned with a shrug.

"You're kidding."

Lola's stomach twisted into a knot. "All we can focus on right now is this: you and Sam are healthy. Beatrice is on the mend. New cars can be purchased."

"I know you're right," Amanda groaned. "I just hate that someone might get away with this."

"The story's not over yet," Lola told her. "If you'd seen what I'd seen over the past twenty-some years of working in journalism, you'd know that at any time, the story could explode into something totally different. Just wait."

Chapter Six

"**A**udrey! Are you coming? If we don't start decorating in the next half hour, I don't know if we'll have enough time." Amanda slid her sunglasses over her nose and crossed her arms, catching a glimpse of herself in the downstairs mirror at the Sheridan House. It was a gorgeous day in late May and the Sheridan House creaked around her, catching the breeze off the Vineyard Sound. She and Audrey were the only ones there, as Grandpa Wes spent the day with his sister, Aunt Kerry, and Max was over at Noah's, who'd agreed to babysit.

Audrey bustled down the staircase, carrying a wide array of feather boas, hats, bustiers, and high-heeled boots, most of which they'd purchased from the local consignment shop the previous evening. On the last step, she caught herself on the feather boa and nearly teetered forward, yelping with alarm.

"Let me help you." Amanda hurried up and grabbed one-half of the mass, laughing. "I told you. We need a better system."

"You and your systems," Audrey teased. "I think we're doing just fine. Let's shove everything into the trunk and head over."

Amanda groaned inwardly as she led her cousin out to the driveway, where they loaded up the rest of the costumes. That night, they'd rented a cabin on the outskirts of Edgartown, along the waterline, where they planned to stage the "Grandest Sheridan Bachelorette Weekend Ever." It was a secret, something they'd concocted with Susan's and Christine's help to ensure that Lola was free and there would be babysitting available for Mia and Max. They'd also invited Charlotte, Claire, and Kelli Montgomery, along with two of Lola's dear friends from Boston, Valerie and Jenny.

Amanda started the engine and began to drive down the driveway in reverse. Her heart pounded in her throat. When her tail traced the edge of the driveway, another car sped past. She shrieked with fear and pressed her foot hard on the brake.

"Uh-oh," Audrey muttered. "This is your first time driving since the accident, isn't it?"

Amanda groaned. "I hate myself right now."

"Just let me drive," Audrey offered.

"You? You barely even know the concept of red lights."

"I view red lights as suggestions," Audrey said with a shrug.

"You're insane." Amanda giggled good-naturedly and forced herself to breathe. "I can handle it. I can't let that idiot destroy my life."

"Yeah! Not another one, anyway," Audrey said with a crooked smile.

Amanda rolled her eyes. "I assume you're talking about my lovely ex-fiancé?"

"No. I'm talking about Ryan Gosling when he had babies with Eva Mendes."

Before Amanda knew it, she'd driven the car from the driveway and pointed them toward the cabin on the outskirts of Edgartown. Her stomach bubbled with laughter as Audrey continued to prattle on, easily drawing her from one topic of conversation to the next. The questions were ridiculous yet easily answered.

"Do you think Ryan Gosling ever misses Rachel McAdams?

"Do you think Selena Gomez is secretly glad that she and Justin Bieber broke up for good?

"If someone had forced you to be famous, would you rather be a singer, dancer, actor, or artist?

Amanda fell into easy conversation with her cousin, one of her greatest friends in the world, as she slowly but surely traced the path to the cabin along the waterline. When she parked outside, she dropped her shoulders forward and breathed a sigh of relief.

"Thank you," she finally said, locking eyes with Audrey.

"For what?" Audrey said in a sing-song voice, despite knowing that she'd gotten them the rest of the way to the cabin on conversation alone.

Amanda and Audrey gathered the decorations and costumes from the back seat and trunk of Amanda's car and headed toward the creaky porch of the wooden cabin. There, they discovered the key under the mat (just as the owner had told them) and entered a beautiful old-world fantasy with large windows that opened onto the Atlantic

Ocean. Frothing waves surged toward them before dangerously dunking themselves along the beach.

"It's perfect," Audrey breathed, closing her eyes as the salty winds came over them.

Amanda began to organize the costumes: the boas and leather jackets and leather skirts and high-heeled boots and silly hats. On top of streamers, giant letter balloons, and gorgeous flowers (which they'd picked up from Claire), they also had a custom-made sign that read:

WELCOME TO THE BACHELORETTE PARTY

IN HONOR OF LOLA SHERIDAN

May 20th, 2022

As they worked, they blared music from the speakers and danced around the cabin, pregaming with champagne from one of the numerous bottles they'd had delivered to the cabin. Bit by bit, Amanda found herself having much more fun than she'd had since the accident. She delighted in how beautiful the cabin looked and the prospect of spending two beautiful days with some of her favorite women—gossiping, eating, and drinking in the spring sunlight along the water.

Amanda set up a dessert table in the kitchen, dotting beautifully decorated cupcakes across china plates. Audrey stepped back into the kitchen, covered in glitter from one of the decorations, and attempted to brush herself off.

"It's no use," Audrey said with a laugh.

"Once glitter is on you, there's no hope," Amanda agreed.

Audrey's smile widened. She poured them a bit more

champagne and then checked the time, reporting that they had a half hour before the guests arrived.

"It's good you pushed me out the door," Audrey reported as she sat across from Amanda, a bit to the left of the cupcakes. "Left to my own devices, I never would have decorated the entire place in time."

For a moment, Amanda and Audrey allowed themselves to admire their work. Amanda sipped her champagne, allowing the bubbles to float across her tongue.

Audrey tilted her head knowingly. "Do you think you'll ever want something like this?"

Amanda guffawed, dropping her eyes to the cupcakes. "A bachelorette weekend?"

Audrey nodded. "Why not?"

"I don't know. My friends didn't give me much of one back in Newark. It was always expected that I would marry early. Chris wasn't a surprise for anyone. Maybe he didn't even seem worth celebrating, either."

"That's mean," Audrey countered. "If I had known you better, I would have thrown you something insane."

Amanda chuckled. "It's true that we didn't get close until after Chris left me at the altar. Thank God for Chris." She lifted her glass in the air playfully, toasting her ex-fiancé wherever he was.

"You and Sam seem really close. Especially since the accident. You've hardly left one another's side," Audrey pointed out.

Amanda puffed out her cheeks. "It seems pretty intense. Different, really, than it ever was with Chris. It's not that I feel this urgent desire to immediately marry him or something. It's like I feel looser and freer with myself and my time and my stupid lists. I mean, the other day, I even let myself sleep in till nine."

"Nine o'clock in the morning? Amanda! You slept half the day away," Audrey teased.

Amanda laughed, genuinely pleased at the differences between herself and her cousin. They brought out the best in one another and would always, as they flourished through their twenties, thirties, forties, and beyond (God willing).

A rap at the front door of the cabin broke their reverie. Amanda leaped up to find Susan and Christine, both dressed up in short skirts, leather jackets, and high-heeled boots.

"Your aunt Christine forced me to put these on," Susan said with a sigh as she stepped in, clopping her heels.

"We're celebrating Lola's last days of being single. You can't do that dressed in jeans and a T-shirt," Christine touted as she removed her leather jacket to reveal a newly cinched waist.

"Christine! You look hot," Audrey cried, leaping up to hug her aunt.

Christine blushed as Susan waved a hand.

"Our Christine used to hate exercise. Now, she refuses to miss a morning of spin class and has even dragged me out for a few classes," Susan explained.

"Endorphins, baby," Christine joked. "Can't get enough."

Susan's lips parted as she assessed the cabin and its decorations. "It looks incredible in here. Truly Pinterest-worthy."

"It was a team effort," Amanda added, smiling at Audrey.

"Who else is coming?" Christine asked.

"Mom's friends, Valerie and Jenny. Have you met them before?" Audrey asked.

"No," Christine replied.

"They're interesting," Audrey stated, tilting her head to and fro. "I think they're left over from Mom's party days. Jenny's an artist, and Valerie's still trying to get her music career to take off. Back in the old days, when Mom was this free-spirited twentysomething journalist, I think their friendship made a whole lot more sense."

Susan twisted her lips thoughtfully. "It's interesting to learn more about the bits and pieces of your lives before we all came out to the island. Twenty-five years add up, don't they?"

At that moment, another knock rang through the cabin. Audrey shot toward the door and opened it to reveal two women in their early thirties or late thirties, both wearing cool and sophisticated bohemian clothing. The blonde on the right tossed her head to allow the ocean winds to course through her curls. The woman beside her had thick eyeliner and jet-black hair and wore a flowing skirt and a pair of pointed-toe boots.

They looked every bit the way Lola Sheridan had two years ago when she'd first arrived back on the island.

"Valerie! Jenny!" Audrey stepped up to hug each of them, the women who'd been her makeshift aunts over the years.

"Audrey. Look at you!" Jenny, the blonde, sounded joyful and easy, while Valerie remained sharp-eyed and fearful, as though she didn't trust the Sheridan women at all.

"Welcome to the Vineyard," Audrey continued, drawing back to gesture toward the decorated cabin. "So glad you could make it to Mom's party."

Valerie stepped through the door, her face shadowed as she nodded to Amanda, Susan, and Christine.

"You're the sisters?" she asked, almost coldly.

"Guilty," Christine replied. "I'm Christine, and this is Susan."

"Susan, of course. The perfect one," Valerie tried. "We've heard about you over the years."

Susan's cheeks burned red with embarrassment. Yes, Amanda's mother strived to be perfect in everything she did. But it wasn't like she liked being reminded of that all the time.

"I'm not perfect," Susan countered. "Far from it."

"She told us all about growing up here on this suffocating island," Valerie continued.

"Valerie..." Jenny warned, closing the door behind her. "Lola's told us how marvelous this new chapter of her life has been. We're here to celebrate that. Remember?"

Valerie scoffed, then reached for a bottle of champagne, pouring the rest of the contents into a glass without asking. "Let's get this party started, shall we?"

Amanda and Audrey eyed one another, genuinely shocked at the coldness Valerie had brought along with her. Was she really that resentful that Lola had left them in Boston?

"Jen, you want some?" Valerie asked.

"We've already cracked a bottle open," Audrey said, her voice wavering.

"It's never too early to pregame," Christine tried. "It's my one weekend off from motherhood. I'm ready to cut loose."

"Motherhood?" Valerie asked with a wry laugh. "I'm starting to think that Jenny and I are the only ones who haven't given in to growing up yet."

Valerie said "growing up" as though it was the most monstrous decision anyone could make. Amanda glanced toward Susan, who sipped her champagne anxiously.

"Even you, Audrey," Valerie shot out. "A baby at nineteen!"

"That's what Lola did," Christine said. "I had a baby in my forties. Just because life happens to you, just because you live, doesn't mean you have to 'grow up' in any sense of the words."

Valerie rolled her eyes as silence folded over the group. Amanda lifted her chin and struggled to come up with something to say, something that would realign the happy mood in the cabin.

"What time did you tell your mom to meet you out here?" she asked Audrey.

"In about a half hour," Audrey returned, crossing and uncrossing her arms. "We're supposed to meet at the far end of the beach. Then I'll slowly walk her to the cabin for the surprise."

"Brilliant," Susan said, trying to find strength in her voice again. "The Montgomery sisters just texted that they're on their way. It'll be a beautiful party."

Valerie knocked the rest of her champagne glass down her throat and rolled her eyes toward Jenny as though to say, *Why the hell did we come here?* Amanda felt suddenly saddened at the fact that Lola had been around such dark personalities for two decades. No wonder she'd fallen back into the warm arms of her Martha's Vineyard family, just as the rest of them had.

Chapter Seven

"I don't want to keep you." Beatrice's voice rang out beautifully, as song-like as a bird. She sat across from Lola at the Sunrise Cove Bistro, her hands wrapped tenderly around a mug of cappuccino and her eyes alert.

"I still have a little while," Lola told her, shoving her phone back into her pocket and cursing her own distraction. In truth, she'd had an absolutely lovely day with Beatrice and Tommy. With Beatrice in her wheelchair, Tommy and Lola had alternated pushing her around Oak Bluffs and describing the history and the way the island erupted with life in the summertime.

"You said you're meeting your daughter?" Beatrice suggested.

"She wants me to meet her at the edge of this beach on the southern part of the island outside of Edgartown," Lola said. "Not far from Katama Lodge, actually." She then leaned forward conspiratorially and whispered, "I think she has a surprise up her sleeve, although I can't be sure. Audrey was always a stellar liar. She gets it from her mother. We're both storytellers."

Beatrice chuckled good-naturedly, the laughter growing louder as Tommy approached from the bathroom.

"What have you two gotten yourselves into?" he asked as he joined them at the table again, his hand around his light beer.

"Your Lola has just been describing her spitfire daughter," Beatrice said mischievously.

"That Audrey is really something," Tommy agreed. "I've had the privilege of watching her become a remarkable young woman the past couple of years. Heck, she's more grown up than me in some ways. I've lived most of my life out at sea, avoiding my problems."

"His mother and I had our doubts about our Tommy," Beatrice continued, mostly to Lola. "We knew it would take a truly spectacular woman to stop him in his tracks. We were never so old-fashioned that we thought every person on earth needed somewhere to call home. We just felt that you know, the love that a partnership can bring to your life is unquestioned. If you find the right partner, that is."

Lola tilted her head knowingly, wishing she could spread out the many stories of this woman's life like a map and chart the course of her years.

"Were you ever married, Aunt Beatrice?" Lola finally asked.

Beatrice toyed anxiously with the edge of the bandage that stretched across her upper arm. "I was. He was the greatest man I'd ever met."

Lola's heart thudded with fear. She could only

imagine the story Beatrice would now tell, about illness or accidents, about loss of life.

But instead, Beatrice continued with a far different story. "In our midfifties, we realized that, although we still loved one another, we didn't feel that romantic love any longer. We were more like roommates or best friends."

"And you decided to part ways?" Lola asked, surprised.

"We did. Our friends thought we were insane. They were like, 'Do you really want to go on a first date again?' And I told them, of course! Why not? It's the only way to learn more about myself. It's the only way to push my story forward."

Lola had never heard this perspective from a sixty-something woman. She arched her brow playfully toward Tommy. "That's beautiful. Isn't it?"

"It's like we've lived opposite lives," Tommy told his great-aunt Beatrice.

"That's not to say I haven't had my heart broken a few times since then," Aunt Beatrice continued with a laugh. "Imagine me learning about the concept of 'ghosting' at the age of sixty-one!"

"Ghosting?" Tommy asked.

"You probably know all about it," Lola teased. "It's when you go on a date with a woman and never call her again."

Tommy's cheeks burned tomato red. "Come on. I was always somewhere else by the next day."

"Men," Aunt Beatrice said with a laugh. "Can't live with them..."

"Well, actually. Apparently, I can," Lola corrected knowingly.

As Beatrice sipped her cappuccino, Tommy and Lola

shared a smile across the table. Tommy took her hand delicately in his across his thigh.

Although Aunt Beatrice pretended not to notice this genuine moment between them, the air shifted. She sniffed and said, "You know what? I think I'm pretty beat. I'll head upstairs to my room if you don't mind helping me up there."

"Of course," Tommy said, jumping from his chair to draw her wheelchair out from beneath the table.

Lola's fingers fluttered against Tommy's as they walked Aunt Beatrice through the Sunrise Cove Bistro, headed for the foyer.

"Hello there!" Sam greeted, adjusting his tie as they approached.

"Hi, Sam! Thanks again for getting that room ready last minute," Lola said.

"Don't you worry about a thing." Sam's smile adjusted itself as he peered down at Aunt Beatrice.

All he could see was the woman in the accident.

"I heard that you called the ambulance for me the other night," Aunt Beatrice said lovingly. "I wanted to thank you."

Sam stretched his palm out across his chest. "I'm just glad to see you're on the mend."

"I am. Thanks to some stellar doctors and some even better pain medication," Beatrice said.

"You'll let me know if you need anything while you're at the Sunrise Cove, won't you?" Sam returned.

Aunt Beatrice affirmed she would, just as the front door jangled open to reveal two additional members of the Sheridan community: Kellan Frampton and Wes Sheridan himself. As usual, they hung binoculars around their necks and looked fresh-faced and eager after a full afternoon of birdwatching.

"Hi, there!" Wes's smile erupted as he took in the sight of everyone. "I just picked Kellan up from high school and took a little tour around the outskirts of Oak Bluffs. The summer birds are back. Next come the tourists!"

Kellan smiled sheepishly, his hair draping over his ears.

"You were out birdwatching?" Aunt Beatrice piped up, her voice still a song.

Wes's eyes danced down to the beautiful woman before him, wheelchair-bound, with her hands crossed over her lap. His eyes widened with surprise. He lifted his hand and tugged at his collar distractedly.

Was he nervous?

"Yes. It's just a silly hobby, really. Something I've taken to in the past few years," Wes explained.

"It's one of my favorite ways to spend an afternoon," Beatrice continued, her smile crooked. "Tell me, have you seen any osprey yet this year?"

Wes's lips cracked open with surprise. "Yes. Kellan and I spotted two a few mornings back, just along the edge of our property."

"They were remarkable," Kellan interjected.

Beatrice lifted her chin to shine her beautiful blue eyes toward Wes. "It was one of the reasons I wanted to interview at a clinic here on Martha's Vineyard. The wildlife is unrivaled. I pictured myself birdwatching in the morning, hiking the natural reserves, and swimming in the Sound as often as I could."

Wes's face grew shadowed with recognition. "You

were the woman involved in the accident earlier this week."

"That's right," Beatrice confirmed.

"I'm sorry, Beatrice. I should have introduced you," Lola stuttered. "This is my father, Wes Sheridan."

"Pleased to meet you. My name is Beatrice."

"I'm sorry to hear that my island didn't exactly roll out the red carpet," Wes offered. "I hope you'll still find it in you to give us another chance."

"The plan was to stay on the island at least until my great-nephew Tommy weds Lola. If I get this job at the Katama Lodge and Wellness Spa, the plan extends a whole lot longer," Beatrice affirmed. "And don't worry. Based on the hospitality I've received over the past few days, I can sense the goodness of this place. I won't rate everything on one experience."

"Beautiful," Wes whispered back, clearly captivated.

Is Dad flirting? Lola glanced toward Tommy, whose eyes were slightly buggy.

"Anyway. We came in for a bite to eat," Wes finally managed, glancing back toward Kellan as though he'd just remembered he was there. "Starving after that walk. Kellan demands an ice cream sundae."

"Grandpa, you're the one who dragged me here for a sundae," Kellan teased.

Sam hurried to set up the ramp that allowed Tommy to wheel Beatrice up to the second floor. Lola carried Beatrice's things delicately, watching the older woman's face as Tommy assisted her. It must have been the strangest thing, handing over your own free will to the first person you trusted.

"Have a good rest of your day, Beatrice." Lola waved from her doorway as the older woman got settled. "If I don't head out to meet Audrey soon, she'll— Hmm. I don't know. What will she do, Tommy?"

"Probably just make fun of you about something," Tommy said with a laugh. "That's typically the Audrey way."

"I can't wait to spend more time with you both," Aunt Beatrice said. "Have a beautiful time, honey."

Lola scampered down the stairs and leaped into her car, grateful for the freedom this afternoon allowed her. As she started the engine, she dreamed up a strange reality— one that involved her father falling in love all over again.

But was it even possible for Wes Sheridan to fall in love? His memory diminished by the day; he was headed toward the darkness of dementia. There was only a question of when he would lose the full depths of his memory, not if.

Still, isn't everyone operating on limited time? Lola and Tommy currently leaped into their lives together in their forties, with the potential for another forty years down the line. There were no guarantees in life. And Aunt Beatrice seemed like the sort of woman to know that, through and through. After all, she'd been brave enough, in her fifties, to start all over again, just because she no longer felt the love she craved. That was really something.

Chapter Eight

Lola parked her car on the southern edge of Martha's Vineyard in a little clearing between trees, where a boardwalk bucked down from the parking lot and down to the whipping sands below. It was a strangely windy day, drawing the winds from the Caribbean all the way up to Martha's Vineyard and warming her cheeks and forearms. Whatever surprise Audrey had planned, Lola was ready to welcome it with open arms— grateful for all she had and all she could build.

When Lola appeared at the bottom of the boardwalk, she found Audrey peering out across the waters, her arms outstretched so that the wind flapped at her sleeves and tore at her dark curls. From a distance, she could have been Lola herself— or Anna Sheridan from the distant past. Lola stretched out her legs to run toward her, the heels of her boots digging into the sands. Audrey screeched out just before their impact, where they turned and turned in circles, laughing like much younger girls.

My daughter. My everything.

When their hug broke, Lola stepped back, ruffled her hair, and said, "Why did you drag me all the way across the island, girl?"

"You'll just have to see," Audrey shot back. "You're always so impatient, aren't you?"

Audrey directed them westward along the beach, stringing her fingers through Lola's and chatting about their days. Max, apparently, had a newfound love for blueberries, which made his tongue look perpetually blue. Lola laughed and described the incident of the meeting between Aunt Beatrice and Grandpa Wes.

"You're kidding," Audrey demanded, her eyes illuminated. "Grandpa was flirting?"

"I know. I don't think I've ever seen him flirt with anyone except my mother in my entire life. But dammit, that tears me up inside. He deserves love just as much as the rest of us. Maybe more, after what Mom put him through..."

Lola and Audrey held their silence for a moment as the waves crashed across the sands. There was nothing left to say. After a moment more, Audrey lifted her finger to point at a cabin in the distance.

"That's where we're headed."

Lola stopped short, eyeing a cabin that she'd never seen before in her life— a windswept place on the edge of the woods with a beautiful view of the southern Atlantic Ocean. It was a strange thing to have been raised on such a small island and not know the ins and outs of every single area.

"Is it haunted?" Lola teased.

"Probably," Audrey shot back. "But that's what you wanted, right?"

"You know me too well."

When they appeared at the front steps of the cabin, the door erupted open to allow music from large speakers to swallow them whole.

"HERE COMES THE BRIDE," bellowed out, an R&B version that Lola had never heard. On cue, Amanda jumped out of the door and started to dance as she placed a large white hat on Lola's head. The door opened wider to reveal Susan, Christine, Charlotte, Claire— and then, in the back of the group, two surprising faces.

Jenny and Valerie, her best friends from Boston.

"Oh my God!" Lola cried, overwhelmed with emotion. She'd thought that Valerie had written her off as "boring and basically married" since she'd told her about Tommy. Jenny had been so busy with work lately that she'd hardly reached out.

One after another, Lola hugged her family members and shrieked with joy at the surprise. "You're kidding me. This is beautiful," she whispered at the decorations: the handmade sign that announced her party, the bubble letter balloons, the beautiful flowers from Claire's flower shop, and the long table of desserts and champagne.

When she reached Jenny, she closed her eyes and whispered, "Thank you for coming all this way."

Jenny eased a hand across Lola's back and murmured, "You know we wouldn't miss this for the world."

Valerie seemed bleary-eyed and sharp-tongued already, the way she was when she was particularly unhappy with her life. Lola had always known to keep a wide berth from Valerie when she got in one of her moods. Susan eyed her as though she was a bomb about to go off.

"Hi, Val." Lola hugged Valerie a bit tighter than the

others, trying to translate that she cared for her deeply but that Valerie needed to behave. "How have you been?"

Valerie shrugged. "Not bad. Got to the island two nights ago and had a wild time with this guy in downtown Edgartown."

Behind Valerie, Susan rolled her eyes into the back of her head. She could practically hear Susan's inner monologue. *Honey. You're in your forties now. It's time to grow up.*

"I think I want to hear that story!" Audrey chimed in, trying to ease the divide between the Sheridans and Lola's out-of-town friends. She passed Lola a glass of champagne and cozied up on one of the three white couches in the living room. "Come on, Valerie. The next two days are all about girl talk. Let's dig into it."

"Yeah!" Amanda chimed in, sitting next to Audrey. "I think all of us have boyfriends or husbands or fiancés. Tell us about your adventures."

Valerie's face lit up the slightest bit. She tipped the rest of her champagne flute back to sip another large gulp. Christine hustled over with a fresh bottle and topped several of the women off, her smile nervous yet endearing.

"I've worked in restaurants too long not to jump when someone's glass is empty," Christine explained.

The rest of the Sheridan and Montgomery women gathered around Valerie as she told the story of two nights before when she'd sat at a wine bar and a handsome stranger had approached her.

"I told myself this year that I was so done with dating," Valerie continued as the rest of the women leaned toward her, their eyes shimmering. "I was done with Boston guys and their stupid sports and their stupid emotional baggage. It was like you had to chase after them to get a second date."

"Ugh. Terrible," Christine said with a sigh. "I have a feeling I dated a lot of the New York City versions of those guys."

"Then you know what I'm talking about," Valerie affirmed, slowly loosening up. "It's enough to really destroy a woman's opinion of herself. But this guy the other night in Edgartown? He just came up to me, complimented me, and asked if he could buy me a drink. It seemed so easy and so genuine. We ended up talking all night long."

"That's romantic!" Audrey cried.

"Valerie..." Lola breathed. "That's an incredible story."

"Who is this guy?" Susan asked, her voice still slightly hard-edged.

"His name is Harry," Valerie said. "He's not an original islander. He came here from the Midwest a few years ago and fell in love with the ocean. He works odd jobs, mostly, which is something I can relate to. Music is my passion, but it doesn't pay the bills."

"It's too bad," Lola offered. "You're so talented, Val. I remember coming to see you all the way back in the early 2000s. You killed it with your band back then."

"The Joan Didions," Valerie said wistfully. "I loved that band. All women. We got buzz around the Boston area but never really found traction, you know?"

Lola tilted her head, eyeing her sisters and her cousins alongside her dearest old friends. Her heart swelled with compassion for each of them. She was terribly grateful that they'd gathered to celebrate her love for Tommy, especially now as they tried their hardest to open their arms to Valerie.

After a brief silence, Lola lifted her champagne glass to toast the women she loved most in the world.

"I can't really translate how strange the past couple of years of my life have been," Lola said. "If you'd told me two years ago that I would move back to Martha's Vineyard, rekindle my relationships with my sisters and father, work as a journalist between here and Boston, and fall in love with a handsome sailor, I'd have said you were insane. If you'd then told me that I would eventually go on to direct a musical for the thespians of Martha's Vineyard, I would have laughed in your face."

Audrey cackled good-naturedly, lifting her glass higher as she said, "You were a brilliant one-time director, Mom."

Lola giggled, drawing her eyes from one woman to the next. "It's an honor to have unique relationships with each of you. I feel so much love in this room. I can only imagine how much eating, drinking, laughing, and conversation we'll enjoy over the next two days. Here's to all of you!"

Together, the group sipped their champagne flutes as Audrey hopped up to dance to the next song that came out of the speakers, "Torn" by Natalie Imbruglia. The others sang out joyously, already tipsy from their first flutes of champagne and open-hearted for the night ahead.

"I'm all out of faith. This is how I feel. I'm cold and I am chained, lying naked on the floor!" they sang out, all mostly out of key but fully emotional.

As the late afternoon drifted into evening, Audrey announced the dinner plans: pizza from their favorite

Edgartown pizza joint, plenty of wine, and an after-dinner "game."

"A game?" Lola asked, arching her brow.

Audrey rubbed her palms together mischievously. "Let's just say that Amanda and I put some real work into this one."

The pizzas glistened with heaps of cheese, round pepperonis, bright green peppers, and black olives, some of Lola's favorite toppings. As she ate, Susan scrunched her nose and removed each black olive, saying, "I don't know how we have the same genes, Lola."

"Lola's always had the wildest taste in food," Jenny chimed in. "Remember when we were ridiculously poor in our twenties? What was it you always ate?"

Lola blushed and glanced down at her grease-laden plate. "I can't believe you'd bring that up!"

"What was it, Mom?" Audrey asked. "I probably ate it, too."

"Your mom loved peanut butter and pickle sandwiches," Jenny continued. "We wouldn't let her feed them to you, Audrey."

"We wanted to spare you," Valerie agreed, her eyes sparkling.

"Mom! Pickles and peanut butter?" Audrey cried.

"Don't knock it till you've tried it." Lola tossed her head back as laughter rolled over her.

"Wow. Our twenties couldn't have been more different," Susan offered, plucking another black olive from her pizza.

"What were yours like?" Jenny asked.

"Oh, gosh. My husband and I had a law firm, two children, and a mortgage. I was busy-busy-busy from the moment I woke up in the morning to the moment I collapsed in bed at night," Susan explained.

Valerie cast Susan a dark look that only Lola caught. Probably, Valerie was judgmental of anyone who'd had sufficient funds during their twenties. To Valerie, if you weren't broke, you weren't living.

"Of course, all that crumbled when my husband had an affair with his secretary," Susan went on with a crooked smile, one that tried and failed to hide the pain of the situation. "What a cliché."

"That's awful!" Jenny cried.

"It all worked out for the best," Susan said with a shrug. "I was supposed to play live-in grandma for my son's children, but instead, I came here and started a new life on the Vineyard. A new life that, incidentally, found space for my old high school sweetheart."

"Aw..." Jenny sighed. "I love those kinds of stories. You found one another again."

"We really did," Susan said, dropping her shoulders forward. "We got married last summer. It was beyond my wildest dreams."

Valerie suddenly turned her eyes toward Amanda. "Was that difficult for you? Watching your mother fall in love with someone who wasn't your father?"

Amanda's cheeks burned red at the question.

"I don't think we need to dig into that," Lola shot out to Valerie, giving her a dark look.

Valerie shrugged as Amanda waved a hand sheepishly.

"No, no. We're all friends here," Amanda began. "To tell you the truth, I've never seen Mom so happy. Our life in Newark had a stressful quality." She turned to face Susan and gave her a warm smile. "Now, you own your own law office, take your own clients, make your own hours, and create space for yourself and your needs. It's a remarkable thing to witness."

Susan's eyes welled with tears. Valerie rolled her eyes back to the ground, sensing that her decision to make someone else uncomfortable had backfired.

What the heck has gotten into Valerie? Lola wondered. *She seems even darker than before, as though the world has poisoned her.*

When Valerie got up to refill her champagne flute, Lola followed her and cornered her in the kitchen. In the next room, Audrey turned up the speakers as she collected the plates and stacked the leftover pizza boxes. As the champagne trickled into Valerie's glass, Valerie's eyes lifted toward Lola's.

"What's up?" Valerie demanded, her shoulders hunched.

"Um." Lola's throat tightened. How could she ask her friend why she was acting like a huge B-word around her family? "I was just wondering if everything was okay?"

"It's all okay," Valerie shot back. "Why? Are you worried because I'm not married with children? Are you worried that I don't have stocks or own property? Are you worried that I'm a washed-up musician at the age of forty with nothing to show for it?"

"Valerie. I don't know what you're talking about," Lola murmured. "I love you and everything you stand for. The fact that you're still pursuing music? It's a beautiful thing, but it's also not surprising. You have so much spirit. It has to go somewhere."

Valerie rolled her eyes back and sipped her champagne as she clunked the half-full bottle back on the counter. "You have to sense that I'm disappointed in you for giving up on your life in Boston."

"Val, come on. I fell in love with someone. Real love. It's beyond my wildest dreams." Lola lowered her voice as she added, "And if you can't get on board with that..."

For a moment, Lola half imagined she would tell Valerie to leave the cabin, to allow her and her family a night of fun and games alone. But before she could, Audrey hollered out from the living room.

"It's time for The Newlywed Game!"

"Come on," Valerie shot out. "Let's go play one of these silly games."

Chapter Nine

"What's The Newlywed Game?" Lola asked, eyeing Valerie as she sat front and center in the living room with the rest of her crew around her. She kept her voice light and electric, despite her simmering fear that Valerie was about to burn the cabin down due to her inner demons.

Audrey shuffled toward her backpack and dragged her laptop out, propping it up on a shelf so everyone could see it. "Amanda and I never thought in a million years that Tommy would agree to it. We approached him in April about the idea, and he was all for it." Audrey flashed her eyes toward the bachelorette party as she brought up a video on the screen and pressed play.

In the video, Tommy sat outside the Sheridan House on the porch swing. He wore his freight windbreaker and had a thicker beard than normal, evidence that this had been taped about three weeks ago. Lola remembered laughing with Tommy every time he'd kissed her because his beard had scratched her chin.

"Hi, Lola." Tommy spoke nervously toward whoever

filmed, his hands on his thighs. "Audrey and Amanda approached me with a radical idea they call 'The Newlywed Game.' Apparently, it's a test to make sure we know each other well enough to marry. I told Audrey that we have the rest of our lives to play stupid games with each other, but she insisted this would make your bachelorette party more fun. So I'm going along with it."

Lola laughed joyously as he fell into his "actor persona."

"Wow. He isn't bad," Charlotte quipped.

"The camera loves him," Audrey said. "To be honest, I think he might have a thing for acting. When we finished filming, he asked us several times if we'd gotten everything we'd needed."

"He is cute..." Valerie murmured, sipping more champagne. "I'll give you that."

"Anyway. Lola Sheridan, my future bride, I've come up with a series of questions for you. For every question you answer correctly, the rest of your bachelorette crew must drink. For every question you answer incorrectly, you must take a drink yourself. Obviously, the point of your bachelorette weekend is to party yourself silly. I hope this game helps you on your journey," Tommy continued on-screen.

"Really, really cute," Valerie affirmed, nudging Jenny with her elbow.

"Let's get started," Tommy began. "Number one. Which Caribbean Island did I live on when I was twenty-two?"

Even before Audrey had a chance to pause the video, Lola snapped her fingers. "Barbados."

"Uh-oh. She sounds sure of herself," Claire said with a laugh.

"The answer is Barbados!" Tommy cried.

The bachelorettes groaned, laughing wildly as they drank. Lola beamed at Audrey and whispered, "This is funny."

"Okay. Next question," Tommy began. "What was the first gift I ever gave you?"

"Oh. Easy one," Lola muttered. "A necklace made of amber from the Baltic Sea."

"The Baltic Sea?" Valerie demanded.

"Yeah. He'd gone sailing there and collected amber," Lola explained. "He shined the amber himself and made a necklace out of it. I keep it on my nightstand because I'm so terrified of losing it."

"The answer, my love, is the amber necklace," Tommy boomed.

"Oh no. We're screwed," Christine offered as she sipped her drink.

"Don't worry. He hits some harder ones later on," Audrey said. "Childhood questions. Stuff like that."

"Uh-oh." Lola wagged her eyebrows. "Lucky for me, I have a pretty dang good memory for stuff like that."

"She really does," Jenny interjected. "We would have been lost without your memory during our twenties."

Lola's heart lifted as she played through Tommy, Audrey, and Amanda's game, which led her down the path of Tommy's life. Ultimately, she missed only four questions, which made the rest of her bachelorette troupe groan and laugh at once.

After The Newlywed Game, Audrey announced a game of "How Well Do You Know The Bride?"

"Uh-oh," Christine said mischievously. "I have a hunch it's about to get messy in here."

"Based on what we just learned about your peanut

butter and pickle fascination, I'm a bit worried about how I'll do on this game," Susan said with a laugh.

"You should be nervous," Valerie touted, arching her brow.

Lola cast her a dark look. *Why are you being so competitive?* She wanted to scream.

"All right. Let's do this," Audrey began, reaching for a large cowboy hat positioned upside down on an empty chair. She passed the cowboy hat to Christine, explaining, "Take a paper, read the question, and answer it as best as you can. If you can't answer it, you drink. If you can, everyone else drinks."

"Here we go," Christine began nervously, unfolding a piece of paper. "What was Lola's first boyfriend's name?"

"Oh..." Susan snapped her hand over her mouth.

Valerie and Jenny exchanged glances knowingly. Lola remembered telling both of them about her past loves from middle school and high school and the fact that nothing had ever "stuck" for her.

"Gosh. That's tricky. I spent most of your early dating years locked in my bedroom," Christine said with a funny smile.

"We know it!" Valerie called out.

"Shh," Jenny hissed.

"Gosh, I'm sorry, Lola. I don't know," Christine finally said with a sigh.

"It was Robbie!" Valerie cried, her eyes flashing toward Lola. "Right, Lola? Robbie? The guy you made out with outside the middle school during third period?"

"I got in so much trouble," Lola affirmed. "But the teachers didn't want to tell Dad what happened. Wes Sheridan wasn't to be bothered during those years. It's why I got away with a lot."

Lola shrugged sheepishly and beckoned for Christine to drink. Christine laughed and passed the cowboy hat around. "I guess we'll learn a whole lot about our Lola tonight."

Charlotte took the hat next, drew a card, and read, "What is Lola's favorite cocktail?" Charlotte puffed out her cheeks in thought before finally saying, "Aperol Spritz?"

"Easy one," Valerie affirmed, sipping her glass. "She's marrying an Italian, after all."

"It's true. I'm borderline obsessed," Lola said, still on edge about the strange glint in Valerie's eyes.

The next questions hit on aspects of Lola's journalism career, Audrey's father, Lola's hobbies, and Lola's favorite movies and books. Lola was overwhelmed with the list of questions and the number of answers her friends and family actually came up with.

"You guys know me a whole lot better than I thought," Lola joked.

A little while later, Susan grabbed a piece of paper from the cowboy hat and read, "Where did Lola always say she dreamed of moving to one day?" All the color drained from her cheeks. "Gosh, I'm not sure I know that one. I hate that I don't know it, Lola."

Lola shook her head, smiling. "Don't worry about it. Things have changed since I got to the Vineyard."

"You're telling me," Valerie interjected.

Lola arched her brow toward Valerie. "What's that supposed to mean?"

Valerie gesticulated toward the cowboy hat. "I mean, Lola, come on. You never shut up about moving to California. It was always the next thing on your lips. You had that 'move to California' fund in your piggy bank. You sang that 'California Girls' song by Katy Perry like, nonstop."

"Terrible song," Lola tried to joke. "I'm sorry about that."

"That's not the point, Lola." Valerie seethed, now, as though Lola not caring about California anymore was a personal affront to Valerie. "You gave up, Lola. You gave up on yourself and your dreams. You let yourself settle for this life on Martha's Vineyard. And I hate to say it, but I can see how unhappy you are."

Everyone was quiet after that. Only the speakers made noise, playing "I Want It That Way" by the Backstreet Boys, which didn't exactly fit the newly sour mood.

"Valerie. Come on," Lola interjected. "It's just a stupid game."

"No. I've had about enough of this," Susan countered, using her "lawyer" voice. "Valerie, I've never met you before. I don't know anything more about you than what you've revealed to me today. All I can say is this. You stormed into our party and acted like a brat the entire time. I don't know why you're so unhappy with your life that you have to ruin Lola's bachelorette party, but I'm telling you now, you'd better quit it."

Valerie's lips parted with surprise. She looked like a young woman who'd just been grounded from going out. Lola dropped her eyes to the ground, her cheeks burning with shame.

For years, Valerie and Jenny were my only friends.

Now, it's like they don't fit into my life at all.

Is that my fault? Did I completely change?

Valerie stood from the couch and stomped toward the kitchen, blaring out, "Jenny, I'm leaving."

Jenny shifted timidly on the couch, clearly on edge

about letting Valerie go alone. She locked eyes with Lola, who nodded and mouthed, "Maybe it's for the best."

"I'll call an Uber," Jenny finally sighed, jumping from the couch to gather her things. "Come on, Valerie."

In the chaos that followed, Lola wrapped her arms around her knees and stared at the fireplace bricks. Backstreet Boys shifted to a song from the early 2000s that she, Valerie, and Jenny had played on repeat back in the old days— "I'm Real," by J.Lo. Valerie locked eyes with Lola as she stomped toward the door. Within her eyes, Lola could feel the density of their time together, along with the anger Valerie now felt because Lola had moved on.

I can't live that life anymore. I'm sorry. Lola wanted to tell her this but instead bit hard on her lower lip and nodded toward Jenny and Valerie as they left. Audrey walked over to the door and watched outside quietly before reporting that the Uber had arrived.

"Do you think they'll be able to find a hotel at this time of night?" Susan asked, always the worried mother type.

"Let's not worry about them anymore," Christine tried, her eyes toward Lola. "Are you all right, Lola?"

Lola shrugged. "I'm so sorry about Valerie. I don't think I knew she still felt so resentful toward me for leaving."

"The woman is in her forties. It's time for her to grow up," Susan countered simply.

"I don't think it's that easy for everyone," Lola offered. "We're all on different timelines, and that's totally okay. I just think she's really unhappy and taking it out on whoever's around. It's a sad thing to see, especially because I really do love her so much. We've been through a lot."

The Sheridan and Montgomery women stared down at the rug between the couches. Lola's heart pounded. It felt as though her "sisters" from her previous life couldn't allow her the happiness of her current one. She felt like she'd betrayed them.

"Let's keep this party going, shall we?" Audrey said finally, smacking her hands together as she jumped up to grab another pre-made game. "If you ladies still have it in you, I have another idea."

From under the table, Audrey procured a ridiculous sight: a cardboard cut-out of Tommy Gasbarro himself, very nearly the correct size and width. Lola howled with laughter, shoving Valerie's darkness from her mind. Audrey positioned the cardboard cut-out against the wall and then passed out little feminine lip cut-outs to each of the bachelorettes.

"This is an old-fashioned game made new," Audrey explained. "Pin the Kiss on the Groom."

"Like Pin the Tail on the Donkey?" Charlotte asked with a laugh.

"Oh yeah. But unlike when we were kids, this time we're all a little tipsier. It should be a good time," Audrey said mischievously. "Plus, I have this blindfold here." She reached into another bag to find a light-pink sleep mask. "Who wants to go first? Amanda? Why do I think you're perfect for this?"

Amanda laughed and waved both hands in front of her face. "No way! I'm so drunk already."

"Come on, Amanda. Someone has to try it," Audrey said, sliding the face mask over Amanda's eyes.

Amanda groaned as Audrey positioned her in front of the cardboard cut-out, where she twirled her in circles. As they watched, Christine slid onto the couch next to Lola and muttered, "Are you sure you're okay? That was kind of brutal."

Lola nodded, furrowing her brow. "I don't want to let her ruin the rest of the weekend."

Christine shrugged. "I just remember being like her, you know, before I met Zach. Before I had Mia. I was so resentful of the rest of the world for moving on. I thought partying into my forties meant I was winning. I was so wrong."

Lola nodded, swallowing the lump in her throat. "Thanks for saying that, Chris. Really. I guess it's something Valerie has to figure out on her own."

Before them, Amanda staggered forward with her fake lips extended, plastering them on Tommy's forehead. When she removed the face mask, she cried out in alarm.

"I was so off!"

"Oh yeah. Absolutely terrible job," Audrey said. "At least you managed to find his face. Who's next?"

The night carried on until around one, when the Sheridan and Montgomery women collapsed in their upstairs bedrooms: Audrey with Lola, Amanda with Susan, Christine with Kelli, and Charlotte with Claire. One bed remained empty, a sight that made Lola terribly sad.

That time of my life is over. I'm welcoming this new era with open arms and wishing Valerie good luck in all she does. It's all I can do.

Chapter Ten

The Sheridan and Montgomery women left the cabin on the southern edge of the island on Sunday morning at eleven. As they collapsed into their vehicles and waved goodbye, they all proclaimed the weekend to be "a huge success." Nobody bothered mentioning the incident with Valerie, and in fact, the events of Saturday had basically obliterated any bad memories— allowing them walks on the sunny beach, vibrant guacamole, margaritas, more soulful conversations, plenty of games, and dessert.

Amanda drove Audrey and the rest of their bachelorette supplies back to the Sheridan House, where they planned to go through everything and recycle what they could. On the way back to Oak Bluffs, Audrey dropped her head back on the headrest and heaved a sigh.

"I hope Mom's okay after that Valerie thing. I wish she would have said she didn't want to be there rather than come and try to blow it up," Audrey said.

Amanda groaned. "I had no idea what to do."

"I just hate that it made Mom sad," Audrey continued. "I didn't want to remind her that building this life with Tommy means giving up her old life."

"I think she's made her peace with that," Amanda assured her. "It's something we've all had to come to terms with since we moved here."

"You're right," Audrey breathed. "We've all made sacrifices. It's just that usually, our sacrifices don't come to the island, make fun of us and our family members, and then storm out in a drunken rage."

"Well said."

Amanda and Audrey unloaded Amanda's car and then waited around for Noah to arrive with Max. Noah had graciously agreed to babysit over the weekend, calling it "guy bonding time." Audrey screeched as she brought Max into her arms and kissed him three times on the cheek. Amanda watched from behind, her arms crossed over her chest.

I have to stop dreaming about having a child of my own.

I have to stop wishing time away.

"What's up, Amanda?" Noah asked.

"We had a wild weekend," Amanda tried.

"So did we," Noah reported. "I mean, come on. We ate mashed peas and corn. We watched Peppa Pig and plenty of sports. We even didn't scream that much!"

"Wow!" Audrey cried. "Not that much! Nice work, Max."

Amanda stepped into the kitchen to pour herself a cup of water as Noah and Audrey continued to dote on Max and each other. Amanda's heart shivered with loneliness. As she reached for her phone, a text message came from Sam— as though he'd sensed she needed him.

SAM: Hi there. Are you back from the cabin?

A half hour later, Amanda met Sam at the sailing docks. She'd decided to dress up a little bit, wrapping herself in a light-yellow dress that tied behind the neck and a pair of light heels. The calm air was seventy-two degrees, and the water frothed gently against the sailboats tied along the docks. Sam stood out at the far end of the docks in a pair of jean shorts and a gray T-shirt. Amanda's heart shivered with longing for him.

When she reached him, she fell into his arms and nuzzled her nose in his chest. His large hand wrapped over her shoulder. For a long moment, they couldn't find words and simply fell into the beauty of being alone with one another at the edge of the water.

"How did it go?" Sam asked.

"Oh gosh. It was dramatic for a while," Amanda explained. "Lola's friends from Boston made a mess of things. I felt terrible for Lola."

"I'm sorry to hear that," Sam said, tilting his head.

"We rebounded," Amanda explained, lifting herself up to kiss him. "I hate to say that I missed you, though."

"I missed you, too." Sam's smile stretched from ear to ear. "I thought we could enjoy this afternoon together on the boat. I figured you're tired of drinking, so I brought some sparkling water, fruit, and juice." He gestured toward his backpack.

"You know me too well!"

Together, Amanda and Sam prepared the boat, quickly untying and tying the thick, scratchy ropes and casting themselves out into the abyss. Amanda lifted her chin toward the sun and closed her eyes, listening to the water as it splashed across their boat.

A bit later, Amanda found the energy to tell Sam more stories from the party. "The life-size cut-out of Tommy was insane. After the first night, we carried him with us everywhere we went and took funny pictures of him out by the beach. Lola carried him around under her arm like a poster. It was hilarious."

Sam laughed good-naturedly. "And the desserts and flowers?"

"They were spectacular," Amanda affirmed, grateful that she dated someone who cared to ask her about stuff like that.

"I'm glad to hear," Sam said. "I wonder what Tommy has planned for his bachelor party?"

"Tommy's more of a loner," Amanda said. "I think he'll probably head out on his boat for a few days and call it his own personal bachelor party."

"I don't blame him," Sam teased. "The Sheridan family can be overwhelming at times."

"Oh, come on." Amanda rolled her eyes off to the mainland.

They passed the western edge of the Vineyard, nearing Chilmark and the beaches she most adored. A heavily forested area had trees wrapped around one another in competition for the sun. And off to the right of this forested area, directly alongside the water, came a dark-red glint.

"Sam, what is that?" Amanda said, lifting a finger toward the trees.

Sam furrowed his brow. "I can't make it out." He directed the sailboat closer to the forest, ducking his chin down as they went.

"Oh my God. Sam. Is that?" Amanda staggered forward so that the sailboat teetered dangerously beneath them.

"Careful," Sam breathed.

"No. Sam. It's the car. Oh my God. Sam, it's the car." Amanda flailed her finger toward the Chevy Cavalier, the very vehicle that had caused the accident and then fled.

Wordless, Sam drew the sailboat as close as he could up to the vehicle, which was pointed face-first in the water with its back end along the beach. From where they were, they couldn't make out the license plate number. Still, it was too much of a coincidence to be anything else.

"This is insane," Sam muttered, easing them toward a tree that hovered out over the water and lassoing a rope to tie them. "We have to call the cops immediately."

"Already on it." Amanda dialed the front desk of the police department, where, yet again, Connie answered and chewed gum into the speaker. "I need to talk to the officer in charge of the hit-and-run accident last week. It's kind of an emergency."

Amanda immediately cursed herself for having said "kind of." This was important, and it mattered to her. She couldn't give anyone the space to discredit her. Not anymore.

Over the next forty-five minutes, Amanda and Sam waited on Sam's sailboat, cuddling one another and eating strawberries until the police arrived. Amanda even fell asleep for a few minutes, adoring the haze of the sun and the smell of Sam's skin. When he nuzzled her and whispered, "Baby, it's time to wake up. They're here," Amanda jumped up and glanced toward a little pathway that led around the forest, where two officers in uniform approached.

"Hi, there!" Sam called, sounding triumphant. "What are the chances of this, huh?"

The officers introduced themselves as Officer Gregory and Officer Freddie Marshall. They were in their midforties and a bit overweight in the middle, with red noses that proved they'd already spent a good deal of the spring in the sun.

"We've got a team coming out to excavate the vehicle," Officer Marshall explained. "They should be able to assess it for prints and hopefully get a read on who might have driven it out here. It's obvious that whoever did this wanted to get rid of the vehicle any way they could without going on the ferry."

Amanda's heart thumped nervously. Sam remained captivated, watching as the officers exchanged words they couldn't quite hear from their stance on the boat. After another fifteen minutes, Officer Gregory called out to them again to say, "If you want to head out, could you drop by the station to give a statement on finding the vehicle later?"

Sam nodded, his eyes widening. "Is the license plate the same?"

"It's been removed," Officer Marshall announced.

"Damn." Sam scratched his head and then repeated, "But it's too much of a coincidence, right?"

"We'll let you know when we know more. An abandoned vehicle like this on Martha's Vineyard is always suspicious, that's for sure," Officer Marshall affirmed. "In the meantime, you two enjoy your day in the sun."

Sam and Amanda exchanged glances. Amanda sensed Sam's desire to jump off the boat and join the investigation if only to make sense of the horrific night they'd shared.

"Thanks again," Sam offered finally, waving a hand as his other latched around the rope, preparing to untie it. Amanda also flung into action, helping them drift off from the edge of the island and back across the ocean.

For a long time, Sam and Amanda remained wordless as they headed back for the Oak Bluffs' docks. Amanda wrapped her arms around Sam's midsection and pressed her cheek against his back, heaving a sigh.

She wanted to say this: We went through a horrible incident together, but we made it through to the other side stronger and better than before. Maybe that's a sign that we're ready to build our lives together. Perhaps that's a sign that we were always meant to be.

But she held her tongue, knowing that words like "meant to be" were very similar to the ones she'd carried as a younger twentysomething, so sure that Chris was the one. Maybe there was no such thing as "the one." Maybe love was a decision, every day of your life, to commit to the person you were with. You couldn't rely on silly concepts. You just had to put in the work.

Chapter Eleven

Max clambered around the living room of Lola and Tommy's cabin, dressed in a diaper and a bright blue T-shirt. His black hair caught the sunlight from the kitchen window, and his sticky hands seemed to touch everything, so much so that Lola finally grabbed him with a wet wipe and cleaned him up again.

"You're always such a little mess, aren't you, Max?" Lola cooed, drawing him up on her lap. He smacked his palms against her chest and gazed at her adoringly. "But you get away with everything, don't you? Just like your mother."

Lola and Tommy had spent the previous evening babysitting Max, allowing Audrey a night off with Noah. Audrey, Amanda, Noah, and Sam had gone out sailing, celebrating the first week of June with champagne and bathing suits and laughter. Lola and Tommy had stayed in for the night, putting Max to bed by seven and then watching a movie, both passing out halfway through and then laughing about it after they'd woken up to the credits.

"Does this mean we're officially old?" Lola had asked.

"I'm marrying you, aren't I? I'm too tired to do anything else but settle down. I'm planning to live out the rest of my life on this couch," Tommy had told her as he'd elbowed her.

"Guess the magic's over," Lola had teased with a sigh.

"Guess so."

But after that, Lola and Tommy had made eyes at one another and fallen into a glorious romantic night, one that had allowed them to sleep long into the morning until Max's babbling from the next room had forced Lola up. Now, Tommy was off to teach a sailing lesson as Lola hobbled through the rest of her babysitting duties. Audrey planned to pick Max up by eleven, although it was no secret that Audrey wasn't exactly the best about sticking to schedules.

At eleven twenty, Audrey finally texted to say that she was on her way. Lola carried Max to the fridge, where she peered at her current ingredients and tried to drum up some ideas for their lunch. Ultimately, she ordered burritos online, along with a big bucket of guacamole and tortilla chips. It would be delivered by noon.

Audrey bustled through the cabin door at eleven forty-five, her eyes drooping low with her hangover and her smile loose and contented.

"There he is!" she cried as she wrapped her arms around Max and turned him around and around. "Thanks a lot for taking care of him."

"No problem, honey. We had a good time," Lola said. "He showed me how well he can walk and make a mess of the house."

"Those are his two main talents right now. That and eating way more food than a one-and-a-half-year-old ever should," Audrey teased as she sat on the edge of a kitchen chair and bounced Max on her lap. Lola watched them quietly for a moment, captivated by the beauty of her only child with her only grandchild. Her heart was full.

"How did it go out on the water?" Lola asked.

"It was beautiful," Audrey cooed. "Just a daydream of a day. Although I have to admit, Amanda and Sam still seem a bit strange and messed up after the accident. They asked me if you'd heard anything more about that car?"

Lola's stomach tightened. In the wake of Sam and Amanda's discovery of the Chevy Cavalier on the western edge of the island, Lola had called the police station almost daily, demanding details. It wasn't all about Amanda and Sam any longer, not now that Beatrice was a victim of the crash. Yes, Beatrice mended more and more every day— but that didn't mean that Lola and Tommy didn't remain angry. The woman didn't deserve this.

"Nothing," Lola affirmed quietly. "There were no prints in the vehicle. Nothing inside to indicate who might have owned it, either."

"Wow." Audrey shook her head. "I think it's tearing Sam and Amanda up inside. It's like this mystery, hanging over their heads."

At that moment, a knock rang out from the front door. Lola opened it to discover a delivery driver wearing a bright red visor and carrying a brown paper bag full of burritos. Lola tipped him for his delivery and then hustled in, dropping the bag on the kitchen table. "Lunch!" she announced.

"You're such a provider," Audrey teased. "Just like the old days, when we ate takeout for most meals."

"Hey. That comment severely undercuts my skills with the microwave," Lola returned as she removed the burritos from the bag. "I could whip up meals in no time with that thing."

"Yes, Mother. You were a brilliant microwave chef," Audrey said, rolling her eyes.

As they ate, their conversation bounced along easily. Lola could always count on Audrey to share whatever feelings lurked in the back alleys of her mind. She supposed having a child at nineteen allowed that sort of closeness. She wouldn't have traded it for the world.

"Sam and Amanda are totally in love these days," Audrey breathed between bites. "I know she was scared when she met him. But she's leaning into it open-hearted these days."

"Does she talk to you about it?" Lola asked.

"Not as much as she used to," Audrey admitted. "She wants her love to be private, which makes sense after what happened with Chris."

"Once you've been burned, you have to protect yourself."

"For sure." Audrey's eyes danced toward Max, where he bobbed around on the floor in front of a tiny fire truck. "It sometimes makes me sad to think that Amanda might get engaged to Sam soon and move into his house. What will happen to Grandpa, Max, and me without her? Left to our own devices, we'll definitely just eat candy and burgers for every meal."

Lola laughed good-naturedly as she placed her half-eaten burrito on her plate. "But what's going to happen between you and Noah?"

Audrey grimaced. "I have no idea."

"Probably Amanda feels the same way about you

right now," Lola offered. "Terrified that you're about to start the rest of your life. Terrified that this cozy world you've built together is about to end."

Audrey slid her teeth over her lip. Her eyes grew distant as she considered this. "I just realized that I sound like Valerie at your bachelorette party."

Lola's stomach tightened. "Gosh. That was so terrifying. All I could think about was the old days when she was my greatest confidant, a woman I could trust with anything. Now, she wants to insult my dearest family members? It's hard for me to wrap my mind around it."

Audrey tilted her head. "I would never go as far as Valerie did that night. But if Amanda ran off the island and went off to build another life, I could see myself getting ridiculous about it. Asking her if I was ever important to her at all."

Lola dropped her chin to her chest. "I know you're right. I've thought about calling Valerie and talking to her. But every time I consider it, I get so angry. I can't overcome it."

A few minutes later, the sound of an engine came from the front driveway. Lola leaned forward to glance out the window as she muttered, "Ah, just the mailman." A moment later, the mailman appeared on the front stoop and shoved a selection of letters into the attached box before waving a hand goodbye. Lola and Audrey waved back.

Lola placed her soggy burrito on its wrappings, cleaned her hands, and stepped into the sliver of sunshine on the front porch. She leafed through the mail as Max sang a song in the kitchen, one that he'd been writing the past week or more. "Da da da da," was what he had so far.

"Oh my gosh." Lola lifted a dramatically large and

thick envelope, upon which the United States Journalism Association had stamped their official mark.

"What's up?" Audrey called.

Lola stepped back into the house with the envelope lifted. All the color drained from her cheeks. "I think this might be important."

Audrey leaped to her feet, scrubbing her fingers with a napkin. "It's certainly big enough to be important. Why don't you open it?"

Lola grabbed a knife and tugged it across the top. She then removed the cardboard certificate within, upon which the USA Journalism Association had written her name.

Lola Sheridan
    A Certificate Of Excellence In The Field Of Journalism

"Audrey!" Lola cried as shock fluttered through her. "This is huge. I had no idea my editor was putting my name in."

Audrey grabbed the attached letter and read it aloud as Lola continued to stand in shock with the thick certificate in her outstretched hands.

"Dear Lola Sheridan,

It is our pleasure to announce that you are a recipient of the Journalism Award of Excellence at this year's United States Journalism Association Annual Gala, which will be held June 11th at the Abigail Adams Ballroom in Boston, Massachusetts."

As Audrey read, her voice bubbled with excitement. Lola leaped forward and hugged her daughter joyously, overwhelmed. On the floor, Max smacked his palms together, grateful that finally, his mom and grandmother had caught on to how amazing he thought everything in the world was all the time.

"This is insane, Mom," Audrey said, grabbing a napkin and dotting it beneath her tear-filled eyes. "But so well-deserved. You worked tirelessly as a single mother and a journalist, inspiring me with your incredible attitude and creativity. I don't even know what to say..."

Lola's heart swelled. "Say that you'll be my date to this thing."

Audrey blinked with confusion. "Don't you want to take Tommy?"

"No way. You were with me from the start of my career. Tommy had nothing to do with all those years back in Boston. You were my real partner in crime, the reason I could do everything I went on to do. If you're not there with me, I don't know who else would go," Lola affirmed.

"It would be my honor to be your date," Audrey beamed, lifting her chin. "I've always felt terribly proud to be Lola Sheridan's daughter. This night will be no different."

"Except we'll need fancier dresses," Lola quipped. "I think it's about time to go shopping. Don't you?"

Audrey shrieked excitedly as Max began to perform his new song again. "Da da da," he wailed as Audrey lifted him into her arms and spun around. His baby laughter welled through the kitchen. Lola collapsed at the kitchen table to continue to nibble at her burrito distractedly, entirely grateful for everything she'd worked so hard for and everything she'd been given. It had all been for a reason. She felt sure of that now.

Chapter Twelve

The morning of June 11th, Audrey and Lola hung their gala dresses in the back of Lola's car, stretching the skirts out across the seats to ensure they didn't wrinkle, passed Max off to Amanda (with copious kisses), and headed out to the Oak Bluffs ferry. There, they parked the car in the belly of the ferry and leaped out into the splendor of the sun on the top deck, where they waved goodbye to the island they now called home.

"I made a list of everywhere I want to eat when we're back in Boston," Audrey said, just as the last of the island dissipated on the horizon line. She leafed through her pocket to grab her phone, on which she'd listed out their favorite burger, pizza, Mexican, and breakfast places in the city where she'd grown up.

"You know we're only going to be in Boston for one night, right?" Lola said with a laugh.

"I've prepared myself mentally for an eating marathon," Audrey affirmed.

"Okay. Let's strategize. Today for lunch, we'll do

burgers and fries. Tomorrow, breakfast so that we can regroup after the gala. And before we leave Boston, we have to decide between Mexican and pizza. Or..." Lola's eyes widened with memory. "That fantastic Chinese place. Remember? With the killer dumplings?"

"Gosh, yes. I can't believe I forgot that place," Audrey returned, furrowing her brow. "Maybe we'll have to have four meals tomorrow before we go."

Lola puffed out her cheeks. "You know that I'm supposed to get married soon, right? And I'm in my forties now, which means my metabolism isn't what it used to be?"

Audrey waved a hand. "Go for a run this week," she said flippantly.

"Spoken like a true twenty-one-year-old," Lola shot back. "Talk to me in twenty years."

"Does this mean you don't want to eat four meals tomorrow?" Audrey asked with a sneaky smile.

"No. Of course, I want that," Lola returned. "I just want to complain about it a little bit beforehand, that's all."

"Fair enough."

The drive from Woods Hole to Boston took about an hour and forty-five minutes, during which Audrey and Lola sang songs, swapped stories, and seemed unable to find even ten seconds of silence. Lola fumbled over lyrics, only for Audrey to pick up the slack— bringing them through genres of R&B, rock, indie, and pop.

"Madonna did it better than anyone," Audrey said with a sigh as the last bars of "Like a Prayer" faded.

"You're so right. Hearing you say that makes me finally feel like I raised you right," Lola teased.

"Finally?"

"I was worried until right now," Lola joked.

Audrey cackled and opened the front window to allow wind to breeze through her hair. It caught Lola's, whipping strands over her eyes and across her cheeks.

"It's funny," Audrey murmured when the first signs for Boston appeared on the side of the road. "Max will never know Boston the way I know Boston. It makes me sad a little bit."

"You're a true Bostonian through and through," Lola affirmed. "Just like I always wanted to be." Lola's throat tightened as she added, "But there's no reason you couldn't build a life here again. Especially if the island starts to feel too small for you. I remember that feeling when I was seventeen, aching to get off the island as fast as I could and go build my own life."

Audrey's cheeks burned. "I recently just told you how angry I would be if Amanda moved out of the Sheridan House. Imagine how mad she'd be if I actually left the island."

"The only sure thing in this life is change," Lola murmured.

"I just want to hold on to this reality a little bit longer," Audrey whispered. "I want Max to be one for another five years. I want Amanda and I to stay up till one in the morning talking about anything and everything as the waves come in from the Sound. I want Grandpa to snore so loudly that we hear it through his bedroom door."

Lola was wordless after that, falling into the poetry of Audrey's words. She could chart the loss of the future based on the losses in her past— her mother, her childhood, Audrey's father. Every loss paved the way for future beauty, but it was often difficult to know how to make space for whatever was next.

"Let's drive by our first few apartments, huh?" Lola suggested, tilting her head knowingly toward Audrey. "Let's take a walk down memory lane a little bit."

Audrey puffed out her lips. "Gosh. I'm really going to need all this comfort food this weekend, aren't I?"

The first apartment that Lola had ever taken little Audrey back to had been no more than a studio with enough space for a bed, a crib, a little table that had doubled for food and for writing, and a coatrack upon which Lola had hung her only coat. Lola had very clear memories of pacing through the night with baby Audrey in her arms, staring out at the darkness of the night and wondering if she would ever "make it" in any real way.

Outside the apartment building, Audrey and Lola were wordless for a long time, watching as the current residents came and went. Most of them were dressed shabbily and were in their early to midtwenties, en route to achieving their dreams, just as Lola had been. One woman, in particular, staggered forward with a baby carrier, talking on the phone with a strained expression.

"She's so tired," Lola murmured. "I can feel it. She's like a mirror image of me all those years ago."

"I can empathize with the baby in the carrier," Audrey tried to joke. "She just wants to scream."

"Oh yes. If she's anything like you, that's true for sure." Lola laughed and traced a strand of hair around her ear. She then pointed at the top-right balcony, which was no more than a foot away from the wall. "Valerie and Jenny used to come over and hang out on the balcony while you and I stayed in the shade of the apartment. They thought I was crazy, having a baby so young. But they doted on you, babysitting when I really needed a break or had to chase a story. In so many ways, I never could have become the woman I am without them, now that I look back."

Lola trailed off contemplatively, feeling Audrey's eyes burning with curiosity.

"Why don't you just tell this story back to them the same way?" Audrey suggested. "I can feel how much they matter to you. Maybe that's all they need to hear."

Lola started the engine again, suddenly anxious to get away from this apartment and its festering memories. Audrey re-buckled her seat belt with a click as they drove back into traffic, easing toward the hotel they'd decided on for the evening.

Once in the hotel room, Audrey and Lola hung their dresses in the closet, freshened up, and headed out for a midafternoon lunch that consisted of burgers, fries, onion rings, and milkshakes at their previous favorite burger place, called simply Robbie's. Together, they sat out in front of the burger place, crunching on greasy fries and watching the Bostonians strut up and down the sidewalk with intense purpose. Years ago, Lola and Audrey had sat outside that same restaurant, but as different versions of themselves. Audrey was often covered in ketchup, mustard, and grease with a big smile across her cheeks.

Now, a much different Audrey sat across from Lola, using a napkin of all things as she chatted to Lola about a current journalism story she worked on for the Penn State University newspaper, which she'd agreed to work at part-time from a distance over the summer months. Lola gave what advice she could yet still found herself amazed at the inner workings of Audrey's mind. She seemed cleverer, more put together, and more creative than Lola had ever been— even on her sharpest day.

As Audrey took furious notes in her notebook, Lola

selected one of the last french fries and chewed at the end of it, watching as a flock of pigeons landed on the nearby sidewalk.

"Good thing your grandfather doesn't live in a city," she said. "All he'd have to watch are the silly pigeons."

"Hmm?" Audrey asked distractedly.

"Nothing, honey." Lola lifted her hair with a wave of her hand and then allowed it to drop languidly down her back.

After a long afternoon of wandering through Boston and working off their burgers, Lola and Audrey returned to the hotel to prepare for the gala. As Audrey took a shower, Lola rubbed lotion across her legs, her stomach, and her arms, dressed only in a bra and underwear and gazing out the window.

It seemed that every street across Boston sizzled with memories of Jenny, Valerie, and Lola from the old days. Lola only had to close her eyes for a split second before images of those long-lost days washed over her. Valerie's laughter had been so infectious, making both Jenny and Lola erupt with giggles of their own.

Before she knew what she'd done, Lola grabbed her phone and texted Valerie.

LOLA: Hey Val. I'm in Boston. Can we talk?

She blinked at the text for a long time, wondering if she should take it back. But before she could decide one way or the other, Audrey emerged from the bathroom, bringing with her a cloud of steam and the sudden, uproarious desire to listen to music loudly as they did their makeup.

"Let's get this party started!" Audrey cried.

Together, Audrey and Lola spread out their makeup brushes, eye shadow palettes, long-winged mascara brushes, and perfume. Audrey flicked through her Spotify to find the perfect playlist, something she'd called "GOING OUT."

"How do you do your eyeliner?" Lola asked, watching as Audrey drew a large wing out from the side of her eye and darkened it into a thick swoop.

"You want a lesson?" Audrey asked, her eyes glittering. "It would really change things up between us, wouldn't it? You used to teach me everything I knew about makeup."

Slowly, with all the patience of the mother she now was, Audrey showed Lola how to draw a wing out from her eye with a steady hand. Lola finished it out and blinked at herself in the mirror, fascinated with the new look.

"You can say it," Audrey teased. "You can tell me I'm brilliant. Come on."

Lola laughed. "I would give you a compliment every minute of the day if I could, my beautiful and talented daughter."

Audrey waved a hand. "Too much! As a journalist, you have to know when to hold back. You should know that, right? You are the recipient of the certificate of excellence at tonight's journalism gala."

Lola's eyes widened as the realization hit her all over again. *This is really my life.*

As they finished getting ready, Tommy called to wish Lola good luck.

"Hi, baby." His voice was so textured and gritty over the phone, reminding Lola of a handsome action star in a bad movie.

"Hi, Tommy." Lola dropped herself on the edge of the bed as Audrey puffed herself with a bit of perfume. "We've had the loveliest day together."

"Uh-oh. With you two up to your own devices, I can only imagine what that means," Tommy returned, his voice sounding playful.

"What on earth are you talking about?" Lola's smile stretched from ear to ear.

"Everyone knows you don't let Lola and Audrey spend the day together without a chaperone," Tommy quipped.

"I'll have you know that we only destroyed one-half of the city today," Lola sassed.

"I can hear the sirens from here," Tommy replied.

Lola dropped herself back on the bed and stared at the ceiling, her heart swelling with love for this man— a man who finally understood her.

"Have a wonderful time tonight, Lola," Tommy said. "You deserve all the accolades in the world. I'm glad that people are finally paying attention."

"I love you," Lola breathed. "Thank you. I can't wait to celebrate with you back on the island."

"I'll be here," Tommy quipped. "Just like I always am, these days. Surprising myself day after day with my domesticity."

Lola giggled. "Domesticity looks good on you, my handsome sailor."

"I think so, too."

Chapter Thirteen

ola and Audrey walked two blocks to arrive at the Abigail Adams Ballroom, the site of the United States Journalism Association Gala. In their black gowns, high heels, and extra layers of makeup, they looked stately and important, forcing people on the sidewalk to give them a wide berth and blink at them distractedly, as though they were minor celebrities.

"And maybe we *are* minor celebrities," Audrey suggested under her breath. "It's not like I recognize every famous person on the street. That's really saying something on Martha's Vineyard, especially in the summer when it's full of actors and writers and musicians."

When they reached the Abigail Adams Ballroom, a woman in her midthirties greeted Lola with a smile and said, "Welcome, Miss Sheridan. We have a seat for you and your plus-one at the head table with the Journalism Association president and three other recipients of the prize." She then pressed her headset to explain to some other person, "Lola Sheridan has arrived. We are in transit."

Lola and Audrey eyed one another sheepishly, laughing inwardly about the evident importance Lola had at this dinner. It was so otherworldly.

The president of the United States Journalism Association introduced himself as Mark Rathburn. He was in his early sixties with salt-and-pepper hair, thick glasses, and an Italian suit that made his big beard look almost sophisticated. His hand was warm and large over Lola's as he smiled and congratulated her on her tremendous accomplishments.

"This is my daughter, Audrey," Lola explained as she stepped from his handshake. "She's a journalism student at Penn State and is really making a mark on the world. I couldn't be prouder."

Mark Rathburn tilted his head knowingly as he shook Audrey's hand, as well. "You know, when I read that article in the paper a few months back about all those deaths at the electrical company, I thought to myself... Sheridan? Another Sheridan? But I have to admit that I didn't put two and two together. Audrey Sheridan actually *is* Lola Sheridan's daughter. I shouldn't be surprised. But I am privileged to sit with both of you tonight."

Audrey's cheeks burned crimson with a mix of embarrassment and pride. Lola's heart swelled into her throat as she watched her daughter take this enormous compliment from such a prominent member of the Boston community.

"Thank you," Audrey finally managed. "You don't know what that means to me to hear."

"I think I do know," he told her. "I remember my first huge story. I broke it when I was a little older than you, living back in Seattle. I felt the importance and the power of my words and fell in love with journalism. The best advice I can give to you as an up-and-coming journalist is to be utterly fearless in everything you do."

"I don't even think she needs that advice," Lola beamed. "She's already charged through the first steps of her career."

"No telling where you'll be in a few years, then," Mark continued. He flashed her a business card as he said, "Why don't you send me an email? Maybe we can help one another in the future."

Audrey took the business card with a shaking hand. She glanced toward Lola, initially shocked, before rebounding quickly and saying, "I'd like that, Mr. Rathburn. Thank you." She then slid the card into her bra, as she had nowhere else to put it. Lola laughed inwardly, knowing that that wasn't the type of thing you did at these events. Audrey would have to learn, but until then, she would be forgiven.

Lola and Audrey sat side-by-side at the head table. Their names were drawn out in beautiful calligraphy on little place cards across their plate. Around the table, other recipients of the award greeted them: two men and another woman, all of whom had brought their spouses for the gala dinner. Two people at the table recognized Lola's and Audrey's names as journalists in the Boston area, which thrilled and surprised Audrey to no end. She squeezed Lola's hand hard under the table, mouthing, "I can't believe this."

"You're a star, honey," Lola whispered back. "It's so deserved."

"You must be proud to be the next Lola Sheridan," one of the men receiving the award that night announced to Audrey.

To this, Lola interjected, "Actually, she's not the next Lola Sheridan. She's the first Audrey Sheridan."

"Well said," the gentleman returned contemplatively, lifting his glass of wine.

The gala dinner was served before the awards ceremony, offering roasted vegetables, a choice between vegetarian lasagna or roasted chicken, fresh breads with pads of melting butter, and several salads upon which roasted walnuts and cranberries were sprinkled. At their table, Lola and Audrey charmed the heads of the Journalism Association and the other honored guests, tag-teaming stories and giggling.

"You two are quite the characters," Mark Rathburn affirmed. "I don't know what we'd do at this dinner without you. And to be honest with you, I've nearly fallen asleep at this table for four years in a row."

"My daughter's always the life of the party," Lola affirmed. "I don't quite know what to do with her."

After dinner and dessert, servers walked through to refill wineglasses and collect dirty plates. Mark Rathburn muttered to their table that it was "showtime," sipped his wine, and headed up to the podium, where he tapped the microphone and made it scream.

"Good evening, ladies and gentlemen of the United States Journalism Association," he began. "It is my pleasure this evening to welcome you to our annual gala, where we honor another year of investigative journalism across the Eastern Seaboard and prepare for another year ahead."

The crowd applauded, glancing toward the head table expectantly. Lola heard her name echoing out from a number of lips. Again, it was such a surreal feeling.

Mark Rathburn continued, thanking a number of his colleagues at the Journalism Association and honoring past members who'd retired in the previous year. He then went on to talk about the importance of women in journalism, saying, "It's only been in the past several decades that women have been allowed to speak their truths across the media, and we, as a culture, are far better for it. Of course, we can pinpoint various women who've pushed this to the forefront— women like Barbara Walters, Ida B. Wells, and Christiane Amanpour. They're some of my personal heroes, adding texture to a male-dominated industry and allowing voices like the one we're about to honor to come to life. But as a male, I don't want to stand up here and talk about women in journalism for too long. I'll leave that to the woman we're honoring first tonight, a woman who has such a whip-smart personality and a clear curiosity and a real sense of style.

"Lola Sheridan began her career at the age of nineteen. At the time, she was a new mother, waitressing tables to pay the rent and using the rest of her time to chase stories and force editors to give her a chance. I remember hearing about her fifteen years ago and thinking, 'Wow. If that woman can do all that as a single mother without any money to back her, I have absolutely no excuse not to be successful,'" Mark continued.

The crowd laughed good-naturedly. Lola felt strange, awkward, listening to this man she'd only just met talk about her as though he'd known her for years.

"In the wake of her first stories, she's written about everything from the women's rights movement to sexual assault in the workplace, to teachers' rights, to fashion icons, to musicians, to crime aficionados across the Greater Boston Area. Her stories are continually bright and electric, intellectual without trying too hard. They're a sincere treasure to read... Which is why we've put together the majority of her work into this book."

Mark lifted a thick book from the base of the podium and pressed it through the air toward Lola. Lola's heart lifted with surprise.

A book? Of all my stories?

It was better than any scrapbook. Audrey gripped her hand adoringly as Mark Rathburn beckoned for Lola to come to the stage. As Lola rose, she forced herself to blink out across the audience and take stock of every shining face, all pointed toward her. They honored every minute she'd ever strived for perfection, every night she'd ever stayed up till dawn writing, and every moment she'd ever cried and thought that maybe it wasn't worth it. As she strode to the podium, her heart pounded with a resounding truth: it actually *was* worth it. Every moment.

At the podium, Mark Rathburn stepped to the side as he continued to applaud, his eyes illuminated. Lola nodded and positioned herself behind the podium, forcing any last fear into the pit of her stomach. What did she care what these people thought of her? She'd already proven herself.

"Good evening," Lola began, her voice clear. "I can't thank you enough for the honor of this certificate of excellence. Now that I'm forty years old, I look back on the past twenty-one years of my career and think to myself: how did any of that happen? Especially to a silly girl with a dream?"

Before her, the crowd laughed good-naturedly, grateful that Lola could joke about herself in a light-hearted way.

Lola knocked her head back to allow her long hair to cascade down her back. "When I was a child, about seven or eight, I had a tape recorder with a microphone attached. I felt like that thing gave me access to another world, a world that was elevated from normal reality. I sat on the kitchen counter with the microphone extended toward my mother, asking her question after question, imagining myself like a television reporter. My mother always played along, pretending to be everything from a bank robber to a weatherwoman to Madonna. She would make up these little characters and answer my questions, making the interviews whimsical and alive. She forced me to consider how to sculpt the interview to make the best story, something that I required in my career."

Lola's eyes watered at the memory. She hadn't actually planned to share those stories with this crowd yet felt the words flow through her, uninhibited. Her eyes met Audrey's over the crowd. They were heavy with tears for the memory of this woman Audrey had never been allowed to know.

"My mother died when I was only eleven years old," Lola continued, clearing her throat.

The crowd seemed unsure of where to look. How could they all collectively handle one woman's intense sorrow?

"But after her death, I carried her with me in everything I did. I felt her at every interview, as I stayed up late to write stories or wait tables, and even as I washed my dishes, usually with tears running down my face. Everything I did, I did due to some belief in a greater mission. And today, here with my daughter, journalist Audrey Sheridan, I feel, finally, that I succeeded. I passed on my mother's love for storytelling, both to my daughter and the Greater Boston Area. And I couldn't be more pleased with myself. I strive to continue to bring storytelling and curiosity to the Eastern Seaboard, no matter the article's contents. The news is ever-changing— but our approach to releasing the truth to the masses never does. Thank you so much."

Lola stepped away from the podium as Mark Rathburn took a few steps closer to deliver a gold-plated award, which was sculpted into an opened newspaper. Lola's name was printed along the base— LORRAINE SHERIDAN, which, she decided then and there, she would never change to GASBARRO. How could she? Her love for Tommy had nothing to do with wanting to remain a Sheridan, to link herself forever to Anna, to Wes, and to their shared past.

"Thank you," Lola mouthed to Mark as the crowd continued to roar. "This is one of the greatest days of my life."

When Lola returned to the table, Audrey flung herself up to wrap her arms around her mother's neck. "I'm so proud of you, Mom," Audrey whispered into her ear. "The life we've had together is the most beautiful thing I know."

Chapter Fourteen

"It feels like a hammer literally fell on my head." Audrey placed her forehead on the cool wood of their favorite table in their favorite booth at their favorite breakfast place in the world, just to the left of her huge plate of pancakes.

Lola, whose own head felt similarly worse for wear, reached toward their communal pile of bacon and crunched the edge. "We really pushed it last night."

"I remember everything until right after Mark Rathburn ordered us a round of tequila at that last bar," Audrey whispered. "As he told me where he thought I fit into the future of journalism."

"Mark was drunker than both of us combined." Lola laughed. "I don't think you have to worry about embarrassing yourself."

Audrey puffed out her cheeks and lifted her head. Boston rain splattered across the window as Lola slid her fork and knife through the pulp of her own stack of pancakes, feeling heavy with a sense of loss. After all, a celebration of something meant that a portion of your life was over. She would never strive in her career in the same way. She would always be known as having "made it."

"Burgers and breakfast," Audrey said sadly as she crunched on a slice of bacon. "What else was on the food list?"

Lola shrugged. "Let's not make ourselves sicker than we already are."

Audrey laughed and rubbed her eyes, smearing her eyeliner. "Maybe instead, we should teleport back to the Vineyard. I'd like to sleep for the next week."

Lola dropped her eyes to her plate, thinking about Boston and the intensity of her love for this city. Her life on the Vineyard was gorgeous, brimming with love. But if she'd taken anything from the gala and the night of her bachelorette party, it was this: Boston had been an integral part of her career and life. She couldn't throw all that away; she couldn't avoid acknowledgment.

"I want to drive by Valerie's place," Lola admitted suddenly, surprising herself.

Audrey arched her eyebrow. "Really?"

"I don't know where to put my love for Valerie," Lola continued. "She and Jenny were my family here in Boston. They basically helped me raise you. In so many ways, I never could have won that award if not for their support."

"I don't know what I would do without so much support on the island," Audrey murmured as she slid a big piece of pancake through the syrup.

"They were my sisters, my best friends." Lola swallowed a gulp of coffee as her mind cleared. "I need to stop by Valerie's place. Ask if there's a way to get through this together."

111

"You want to just drop by? No calling?" Audrey asked.

"According to my phone, I texted her three times last night, with no answer," Lola returned sheepishly.

"Oh no. Drunk texting your ex-best friend?" Audrey scrunched her nose.

"I know. Not a good look," Lola replied.

"I guess dropping by is the only way to go, then." Audrey fell back against the cushion of the booth. "Do you think she'd be willing to come with us to the pizza place? Or would she rather hit up the Chinese place?"

Lola laughed good-naturedly, grateful as ever that Audrey was willing to make a joke. "Unfortunately, I don't think this conversation can be food-based."

Audrey groaned. "If you say so."

For the previous ten years, Valerie had lived in a little apartment building about fifteen minutes away from where Lola's last Boston residence (which she'd finally given up about six months after she'd officially gone to the island). Lola drove the familiar route toward the apartment building as Audrey texted Noah in the front seat, laughing to herself about whatever inside joke they shared.

Once outside the apartment building, Lola shut the engine off and traced a path with her eyes to the first-floor apartment, which she and Audrey had traced time after time en route to Val's place.

"You want to come with me?" Lola asked.

Audrey nodded. "I'll be your backup."

"This isn't, like, a mafia thing, Aud."

"Whatever you say," Audrey offered with a crooked grin. Lola laughed, despite everything.

Once outside, rain flattened itself across her forearms

and upper forehead. Lola rustled her fingers through her greasy hair, wishing she'd bothered to scrub her scalp in the shower that morning rather than opting for a "rinse off."

Valerie's front door was just as nondescript as the other apartment doors, with only the number 144 proof that this was, in fact, the place Valerie had resided for ten years. Lola rapped on the front door, shoving away memories about Valerie's horrendous attitude at her bachelorette party.

Hurt people hurt people.

But a split second later, a man in his thirties with a cereal milk stain on his T-shirt answered the door. With a funny jolt, Lola thought, *Is this Valerie's new boyfriend? This milk-stained thirtysomething?*

"Hi!" Lola began, using her half-flirtatious voice.

The man dotted his fingers around his lips, trying to clean himself up. "Hello?" His eyes scanned from Lola to Audrey, who hung back, shifting her weight on her feet.

"Sorry to drop by like this," Lola began, her head pounding with her hangover. "But I wondered if Valerie is around? I'm an old friend, and I really need to speak to her."

The man scratched his bald spot and shook his head. "Valerie? Hmm. Yeah, that's the woman I'm subleasing from, I guess?"

Lola's stomach twisted. "She's not here?"

The man shook his head. "No. I've lived here for about five months now."

"And you have no idea where she is?"

The man bristled. "I guess if I did, I wouldn't feel right about telling you that."

"Listen, dude. My mother is Valerie's best friend," Audrey shot out.

Lola whipped a hand out as her smile widened. "Audrey, it's okay. I respect that. Thank you."

The man shrugged and stepped back, opening the door just the tiniest bit. Through the crack, Lola could make out all of Valerie's old furniture and hung photographs and paintings, proof that most of Valerie's life remained within those walls— the only thing missing was Valerie.

What the heck is going on? And why didn't she mention that she'd moved somewhere else?

Once back in the car, Lola started the engine and allowed it to purr beneath them. Audrey buckled her seat belt and crossed her arms. "Does this mean we should give up?"

"Not yet," Lola murmured. "I want answers. And another cup of coffee."

"Coffee, yes. And maybe a hair of the dog situation," Audrey mumbled. "My head is threatening to explode."

"We can get you a Bloody Mary in a little while," Lola countered as she eased the car from the side of the road. "Can you do me a favor? Can you get Jenny on the phone?"

Audrey breezed through Lola's phone passcode (something Lola didn't know Audrey knew so well) and called Jenny. With the phone on speaker, each ring echoed through the little car until Jenny's eventual answer.

"Hi, Lola." Jenny sounded slightly stricken. "I can't talk right this minute, but can I call you back after my shift?"

"So you're at the coffee shop this afternoon?" Lola

breathed, relieved. She'd thought that Jenny normally worked most Sundays, a paycheck that helped her continue with her art career.

"Just like always," Jenny affirmed. "You in town?"

"I'm going to stop by," Lola offered.

"Great." Jenny's voice was high-pitched.

"Unless that's not something you want? After what happened on the Vineyard, I mean," Lola tried.

"Lola, we've been through so much together. Even though we've been distant lately, it doesn't mean..."

Next came the sound of someone at the coffee shop, demanding why Jenny wasn't paying attention to them. "I've been waiting in line for, like, five minutes. I need a latte to go. ASAP."

"I'll see you in fifteen, Jen," Lola interjected.

"Yeah. See you in a bit." Jenny hung up to tend to the customer as Lola and Audrey continued to creep through Boston traffic.

"You think Jenny will know where Valerie is?" Audrey asked.

"I can only assume so," Lola tried. "Although who knows what happened after their stint on the Vineyard a few weeks back. Maybe our entire three-woman friendship has exploded. If today doesn't work, maybe it's a sign that I really need to move on."

The coffee shop where Jenny worked part-time at was called The Boston Bean. Lola had spent countless Sundays at the corner table, her glasses over the bridge of her nose and a half-eaten scone on a plate as she'd typed article after article. Jenny had always given her refills of coffee, extra snacks, and a listening ear when Lola got lost in the chaos of her head. All that had been years ago by then. Lola's heart craved the intimacy of that friendship. She craved a home she no longer had.

Lola and Audrey stepped into the coffee shop to find Jenny in the throes of a Sunday rush. Lola and Audrey sat their hungover bodies at the same corner booth Lola had always called her own, waiting until the line diminished. When it finally did, Jenny came to their table with two lattes and two scones, set them in the center of the table, and said, "It's good to see my Lola back in her booth."

Lola's chest felt tight. "Jenny. It's so good to see you." She lifted up to hug her, dropping her chin on Jenny's shoulder.

Jenny held the silence for a moment, clearly feeling complicated about Lola's spontaneous meeting. When she stepped from the hug, she sniffed and said, "To what do I owe this pleasure?"

"Mom was given a certificate of excellence in journalism last night," Audrey explained as she tore through the edge of her scone.

"Wow. That must have been amazing." Jenny's eyes widened. "I can't imagine what that must have felt like, Lola. So well-deserved after so many years of hard work."

Lola's cheeks burned. "I know that I have both you and Valerie to thank for that. You were there for me in everything I did. And I'm starting to feel that my running off to the island was more of an abandonment than I realized at the time. I was caught up in the drama of my family coming back together again, and I forgot to honor the family I'd built here."

Jenny dropped her eyes to the table. "Thank you for saying that. You know that Valerie's and my families aren't out here on the East Coast. We've tried our best to support one another, but…"

Jenny turned to greet three new customers as they entered, moving behind the counter to prepare their coffees and platters of snacks. Lola and Audrey continued to nibble at their scones distractedly.

When Jenny returned, Lola placed a hand over hers and said, "I'm just so sorry that I haven't been here. I'll never forgive myself."

Jenny's cheeks lost their coloring. "We'll always love you, Lola. We want to be in your life. That's all."

Lola sipped her latte as she drummed up the courage to ask the next thing.

"I haven't been able to get ahold of Valerie," she continued.

Jenny's eyes grew shadowed. "Yeah. I don't know if she wants to talk to you."

"And I get that. I just wish I could talk to her and explain my side. I wish we could open up about what's going on in each other's lives. But just now, I tried to stop by her place, and some other guy is living there?"

"You stopped by?" Jenny's eyes bugged out.

"She wouldn't answer me. I thought it was the easiest way," Lola admitted. "But then some stranger opened the door and said he's subleasing from her and that he wouldn't tell me where she is."

Jenny's hands searched around the pocket of her apron distractedly. "I don't know if she wants me to tell you this. But you know what? I'm worried about her, too."

"What do you mean?"

"Money's always been tight for Val," Jenny continued. "Like, remember when you and I were just scraping through in our twenties? That's how Valerie has lived her entire life. I think it must be exhausting for her. Like she never feels good enough or smart enough or rich enough to survive."

Audrey pressed her hand against her cheek. "So she couldn't afford the apartment anymore?"

"She crashed with friends for a while," Jenny affirmed. "She was with my boyfriend and me for about two weeks, but it got to be too much. I hated that I had to ask her to leave, but she understood. Now..."

Her eyes dropped toward the ground. Lola's heart surged with fear. Now? What the heck did 'now' mean?

"Remember that guy she met on the Vineyard?" Jenny continued.

"What?" Lola demanded.

"You know. That guy she met at the wine bar in Edgartown. Harry something," Audrey said.

"That's right." Lola half-remembered the image of Valerie in conversation with the Sheridans and Montgomerys, relating this beautiful moment when a decent man had bought her a drink. "You think she's with him?"

Jenny scrunched her nose. "The thing is, Valerie refused to leave the Vineyard after your bachelorette party."

Lola's jaw dropped. "Are you kidding? She's been on the island the entire time?"

"I don't know. She answers my texts and calls but is really cagey about details. I assume she's still with him somewhere on the island, but I can't be sure," Jenny returned.

Lola felt gobsmacked. "And you can't tell me anything else about him?"

"I don't know." Jenny furrowed her brow, removing a wrapped straw from her apron. "He's a guy called Harry from the Midwest, living on Martha's Vineyard. That's all

I can really remember right now." She then yanked herself toward the front door of the coffee shop as she said, "I'll be right there!" to a line of eight impatient customers.

In the silence that followed, Lola and Audrey looked shellshocked. After nearly two minutes, Lola shook her head ominously and said, "She's been on the island the entire time?"

"I don't know what to tell you," Audrey returned. "But with that journalistic head of yours, I have a hunch you'll be able to find this mystery man."

"I hope so." Lola traced a strand of hair around the back of her ear. "I just don't think she wants me to chase after her this time. Maybe, as a journalist, I also have to learn when to stop running."

Audrey draped her hand over Lola's. "All you can do is let her know how much you still care."

Lola nodded, drew her phone from her pocket, and typed a message.

> LOLA: Hi Valerie.
>
> LOLA: I guess you can tell from my many text messages last night that I'm very hungover today.
>
> LOLA: I hoped to catch you while I was in Boston, but I heard a rumor that you skipped town.
>
> LOLA: Please know that I'm always here for you, even if I sometimes don't show it.
>
> LOLA: Love you forever, Val.

Chapter Fifteen

"Amanda. I got your chicken avocado salad." Bruce Holland appeared at the doorway of Amanda's office, lifting the brown paper bag of Amanda's Tuesday lunch through the air. Amanda's morning and early afternoon were heavy with meetings, so much so that her traditional Tuesday walk and lunch with Sam had been canceled. Lucky for her, their colleague, Bruce, had slipped out for salads, sandwiches, and Diet Cokes— the trifecta of fuel they required to get through the end of the day.

"Bruce, you're a godsend." Amanda leaped up and walked shoeless to the door to collect the salad. "How is it out there?"

"Just another beautiful day in June on the island of Martha's Vineyard," Bruce teased, his smile crooked. "While we're locked away inside, doing our best to represent the criminals of the Eastern Seaboard."

"Well said." Amanda grinned, then stepped back as she assessed the contents of the bag.

"Oh. Amanda." Bruce snapped his fingers. "I almost

forgot. I was curious if you could head over to the police station this afternoon to collect some police records for your mom and I. Susan mentioned it this morning, but I forgot to pass along the request. I'd do it myself, but I have a three-hour meeting from one thirty to four thirty."

"You mean, walk from the office to the police station in the sunshine?"

"I do indeed."

"It's a deal," Amanda affirmed.

"You're a lifesaver," Bruce returned, rapping his knuckles against the doorframe. "Having you and Susan around is like having two of the most organized and whip-smart individuals in your corner. I've even started eating more salads since I got here, which has shocked my girl-friend to the core."

Bruce adored namedropping his girlfriend, Elsa Remington, who was head of PR over at the Katama Lodge and Wellness Spa. They'd gotten together the summer before and had a blissful romance, one that Amanda practically watched play out across Bruce's joyous face.

"I told Elsa that we can't eat too many salads at home, though," Bruce continued. "Because if I eat too much greenery, I'll turn into a rabbit."

"You're funny." Amanda waved just before Bruce disappeared into his office, then stepped back toward her desk. There, she tore through her chicken and avocado salad and finished up the notes from her previous meet-ing, grateful for nourishment and the organizational stylings of three different colors of pens.

At two forty-five, Amanda managed to slip out of the office and head over to the Oak Bluffs Police Station. An eggshell-blue sky belled over her, cloudless, and tourists burst in front of her on the sidewalk, forcing her to dally in the warm sunshine. Amanda couldn't have cared less. She even half considered calling Sam to see if he had time to grab an ice cream cone but then remembered that he'd agreed to pick up a shift at the Sunrise Cove Inn that afternoon. Natalie had a doctor's appointment.

This was just Sam's way. He loved helping people out when they needed it.

Connie worked the front desk of the police station, clacking her gum and rolling the telephone cord around and around her finger. It took her a full minute to realize Amanda had stepped through the door, which eventually led her to jump up from her chair and bustle around as though she suddenly wanted to look busy.

"I just need some files for clients of the Sheridan Law Office," Amanda finally explained. "I'll need to make copies if your copy machine is working again?"

The last time Amanda had been at the police station for this very task, the copy machine had been broken. Luckily, Connie reported that they'd recently purchased a new one.

"I have no idea how to work it, though," Connie said, throwing her hands in the air. "So that's up to you."

Amanda had never met a technology device that she couldn't manage to figure out. As she read through her mother and Bruce's clients' paperwork, she slipped each page into the machine, which eventually, after several failed attempts, spit out page after page of copies. In the next room, Connie listened to talk radio and filed her nails, uninterested in how long Amanda took to copy everything.

Which eventually led Amanda to do something she wasn't entirely sure she should.

Amanda flicked through the files, on the hunt for the hit-and-run case from the previous month. As Martha's Vineyard was a teensy place, with few accidents and few crimes, it didn't take long to stumble into it. The file itself was thin, with testimonies from Amanda, Sam, and Beatrice, along with a description of the accident site. Amanda's heart pumped strangely as she read about the Chevy Cavalier that had ripped out of sight. Another page listed the original owners of the Chevy Cavalier, who'd reported their vehicle as stolen more than a week before the crash.

Recently, Amanda had told Sam, "It just bothers me that people can get away with something like that. I thought we lived in a better world. I thought we lived in a place of justice and rules."

To this, Sam had hugged her gently and whispered, "We live in a world of cruelty and jealousy, which is why I thank God every day that we found one another."

Across everything Amanda read in that file that afternoon, she found no new information. She predicted that the police wanted to give up the case. After all, nobody had died. Nothing terribly dramatic had happened. Still, whoever did this remained on the loose. It bothered Amanda to no end.

* * *

Amanda returned to the Sheridan House at five thirty. There, she changed into a pair of shorts and a white T-shirt and sat out on the back porch swing, which creaked beneath her as she swung. An unopened book sat in her lap expectantly, even as her eyes danced across the horizon of the Vineyard Sound.

"Wes! Did you see that?" An older woman's voice rose out from the tree line.

Amanda lifted herself up from the swing to catch a glimpse of an older woman with a cane, a pair of binoculars lifted toward the sky. After a moment, Grandpa Wes shuffled out from the trees excitedly, his own binoculars pressed against his eyes. Amanda followed their gaze toward a glorious osprey, which lifted up from the water and eased toward the clouds.

It truly was spectacular.

After the bird disappeared, Grandpa Wes and Beatrice dropped their binoculars back to their chests, gripped hands, and laughed with excitement.

"We can't be too loud!" Beatrice hissed after that. "We'll chase the rest of the birds away."

"I know. I know. I just can't contain my excitement," Wes returned, his hand still latched around hers. "I wish Kellan could have seen her."

"Me too. But it's just like I told you. He needs to spend more time with guys his own age. Otherwise, he'll never really figure out who he is," Beatrice offered kindly.

Wes bowed his head knowingly. "I'm glad I have another friend as interested in bird watching as me, Beatrice."

From where Amanda sat, she could make out the ruby-red tint of Beatrice's cheeks. Amanda could hardly breathe, as she didn't want to give herself away for spying. After another moment more, Grandpa Wes pointed himself back into the woods between the Frampton and Sheridan Houses and hissed, "Come on. It's a bit cooler now. The birds will be more active. The trail over here should be safe for your cane."

"It's just fine," Beatrice affirmed, walking confidently

behind him. "I'm just so glad to be out of that stupid wheelchair."

"I've had my fair share of time in a wheelchair," Grandpa Wes returned. "I wouldn't wish it on anyone. It's like you're trapped."

Amanda remained on the edge of the porch, watching as they slipped deeper into the woods. The noise of their conversation diminished, as well, leaving Amanda only in the comfortable silence of the Sheridan House— a silence that wasn't truly silence, with its creaking floorboards and its screeching porch swing.

Was it possible that Grandpa Wes was courting this woman?

Amanda dropped back on the swing, pressing her hand across her heart. Seeing the two together made her heart swell with happiness.

"Is anyone here?" Sam's voice rang out from the back of the Sheridan House.

"On the porch!" Amanda called.

Sam's strides made the inner house creak. When he appeared in the crack of the doorway, he came wine bottle first, Sam second. His smile was crooked and endearing, only faltering when Amanda leaped up to kiss him.

"Are you the only one here?" he asked, genuinely surprised.

"I know. It's crazy," Amanda returned, drawing him toward the swing and then pointing his attention toward the waterline, where Beatrice and Wes re-emerged to scour for birds. "But there's a really beautiful reality television show playing down there."

Sam laughed as he uncorked the wine bottle. "You're kidding. What's the show called?"

"It's called *The Bird Watchers: Are They Looking for Birds? Or Each Other?*"

"It's a long title," Sam affirmed. "We need something catchy like Below Deck or Selling Sunsets."

"Okay. What about Lovewatching?"

"Not bad," Sam said, still laughing. "Think it's okay that your grandfather doesn't know he's on a reality television show?"

"I think it's better we don't tell him. It could go to his head."

Sam passed Amanda a glass of wine, and together, they burrowed close, cuddling as they watched Grandpa Wes and Beatrice lift their fingers toward the sky and point out bird after bird. Amanda's heart seized with longing and gratefulness.

Everyone deserved a love like this, she thought.

Chapter Sixteen

It wasn't a difficult thing for Lola to discover the whereabouts of Valerie's new islander boyfriend, Harry. The journalistic efforts involved a simple question at the local Oak Bluffs bar, which led to a conversation with another local who mentioned, "That guy who fixes the roads. His name is Harry, and he has a Midwestern accent if I've ever heard one."

The Tuesday after her arrival back from Boston, Lola searched online for the street address of Harry Billson, a man who lived on the outskirts of Oak Bluffs. The site allowed for a satellite image, one that brought a digital Lola directly to the street alongside the brick house, where a large fence separated the street and Harry's property. There was no telling if that fence was Harry's decision or someone else's. That said, it certainly kept any prying eyes out.

Lola studied the street address as her heart jumped into her throat. *That's where Valerie lives. No more than a fifteen-minute drive away.*

But she doesn't want anything to do with me.

I have to respect that.

I have to let her live however she wants, just as she's allowed me.

"What's up?" Tommy stepped out of the shower, a towel wrapped around his waist.

Lola groaned. "I figured out where Valerie lives. It's not far from here." She splayed her fingers over her eyes.

"And you want to go over there and make everything better?" Tommy sounded matter-of-fact.

"I want to. More than anything in the world. But she wants to build a new life with this guy. If Jenny's correct, Valerie hasn't exactly had an easy go of it the past six months or so. If she's found happiness, I have to respect that."

Tommy clucked his tongue as he pressed at his flowing wet hair, flashing droplets across the wall. "You sound very unlike any Sheridan woman I've met."

"Very funny." Lola stuck out her tongue. "Because we're all so damn nosy?"

"Something like that," Tommy returned with a mischievous smile as he headed toward the bedroom. "Speaking as a loner myself, I can only say Valerie probably appreciates the time you're giving her. Sometimes, people need solitude."

Lola's stomach twisted as she leaned back in her chair, contemplating this advice. She then grabbed her phone to text the other "former loner" she knew, Christine, for verification.

> LOLA: Hey Chris! I have a bit of a complicated situation over here. I just learned the identity and the location of Valerie's new boyfriend here on the island. I can only assume that Valerie's living there with him, only fifteen minutes away. All I want in the world is to talk to her.

Lola staggered to a stop, puffing her cheeks out. How could she describe what she needed to know without insulting Christine?

> LOLA: Tommy says that I should give her space to think. Naturally, as a Sheridan woman, I don't want to give her even a second to herself. Tommy suggests that all Sheridan women are just too nosy— but I have to admit, I don't think that's part of your game.
>
> LOLA: What's your advice?

Christine wrote back a few minutes later.

> CHRISTINE: OMG, look at this milk spill I got all over the couch.

Lola laughed at the photo Christine sent, which featured a screaming Mia and a bunch of milk across three cushions. The white liquid bubbled and soaked into the couch. It brought Lola all the way back to her early days with baby Audrey, scrambling around with a baby and a stupid dream of being a journalist.

> CHRISTINE: Pumping will be the death of me, I swear.

CHRISTINE: But anyway, back to your question.

CHRISTINE: During my very, very lonely times, I was so sure I was a loner. That I didn't need anyone. Not to put Tommy on the spot, but I'm pretty sure the proof that the "loner" lifestyle isn't for him lies in the fact that he's marrying you THIS WEEKEND. Full stop.

CHRISTINE: My point? Sometimes, people don't know what they need. I certainly didn't. If you had asked me two years ago, I'd have told you that all I wanted to do was get drunk with my stupid New York City boyfriend, Frank, and make pastries for celebrities. Compared to my milk-stained reality, it sounds so glamorous. (LOL. Not.)

CHRISTINE: If Valerie's "show" at your bachelorette party told me anything, it's that she needs you, probably a whole lot more than she wants to admit.

* * *

That Friday, June 17th, was Lola Sheridan and Tommy Gasbarro's wedding rehearsal dinner. They decided that the women would prepare for the night ahead at Susan's house, a sort of kick-start to the weekend that included plenty of bubbling champagne, beautiful bouquets, little snacks, and music. Susan opened all the doors of the house to allow the breeze to bluster in from the Vineyard Sound, and the smell of lilacs enveloped the home. Lola sat at the edge of one of Susan's couches, cupping her elbows nervously as Christine went through Lola's makeup bag, hand-selecting their essentials for the night.

"You look white as a sheet," Christine noted when she lifted her eyes toward Lola's.

Lola shivered. "I don't know what's gotten into me. Since Tommy and I got engaged, I've been full-speed ahead."

"Minus that interruption with the blizzard," Christine reminded her.

"Yes. Minus that." Lola bit down on her lower lip and glanced toward the far wall, where a photograph of Susan, Christine, Lola, and Anna hung. The photo of the four original Sheridan women had been taken in 1995, the year Lola had lost her front teeth. She looked silly and sweet.

"It's her, isn't it?" Christine murmured, glancing back toward the photograph. "I think it hung heavily on Susan when she married Scott, too."

"It's just so strange that we're all back. We're all still here. And I still half expect her to find a way back into our lives," Lola whispered. "Like that nightmare will reverse itself, and we'll all just get to live out the rest of our days here."

Christine jumped onto the couch next to Lola, sliding a hand over Lola's smooth hair and holding her in a nourishing hug. After they shared a long sigh and a moment of silence, Audrey leaped through the back door dressed in nothing but a swimsuit and a pair of tennis shoes. A hand lifted, she hollered, "There she is! The bride!" and leaped onto the couch next to Christine and Lola, miscalculating their sorrowful hug as a joyful one.

Lola took this opportunity to brighten her emotions.

"Are you wearing that tonight, Maid of Honor?" Lola teased.

Audrey giggled and glanced down at her bare midriff.

"I thought I'd give the people what they want." She then tugged at a tiny bit of skin, leftover and sagging from her pregnancy. "How do you get rid of this?"

Christine laughed. "Talk to me when you've had a baby after forty." She patted her own stomach, which looked tight under her shirt yet was, apparently, a bit of a mess up close. "Not that it wasn't worth it."

"Always worth it," Audrey returned. "RIP my beautiful bikini body."

"All bodies are bikini bodies." Amanda stepped out of the kitchen with a carrot stick raised, heavy with hummus.

"I think we'd better get ready to go!" Susan hollered from the top of the staircase before emerging in her off-the-shoulder dark-purple dress that shimmered around her knees. Her makeup was sublime, her hair styled in a half updo, and she'd donned a beautiful golden bracelet, which caught the light from the hazy afternoon.

Lola's dress for the evening hung in Susan's guest bedroom. It was ivory and up to her neck, cutting off at the knees to allow her to wear her signature bohemian boots. Christine followed her to help with makeup, suggesting they do something a bit more out there and in your face that evening to contrast with the more subdued bridal makeup of the following day. As Christine styled her, she closed her eyes and lost herself into the beauty of the music Audrey played on the surround-sound speakers.

The rehearsal at Grange Hall would begin at five o'clock in the afternoon. Susan drove Lola, Christine, Audrey, and Amanda in Scott's truck, as Scott was off the island that evening to take care of some freight line duties.

"He'll be back tomorrow, though, won't he?" Lola asked, suddenly worried that a puzzle piece of the family wouldn't be there for their big party.

"You can't keep Scott away from a party," Susan affirmed as she escalated the speed, pushing them faster toward Grange Hall. "He's supposed to be on the island by six in the morning if you can believe it. Kellan's with him, too. Working odd jobs on the freight liner this summer for extra cash. The poor kid! Waking up at four in the morning with his dad."

"I wouldn't be able to manage it," Audrey offered.

"But you have to wake up all the time for Max," Amanda pointed out.

"True. But we just hang out in the warmth of my bed, relaxing. Not out on the Sound somewhere, freezing our butts off," Audrey countered.

The Sheridan women bubbled with laughter and conversation all the way to the gorgeous Grange Hall, the site of tomorrow's wedding. Audrey leaped from the truck and lifted a hand to help Lola down to the sidewalk below.

"I don't need as much help today," Lola said. "But tomorrow, with that long skirt—"

"I'll be your guide," Audrey offered mischievously. "Don't you worry about a thing."

Several members of the Sheridan and Montgomery families had arrived for the rehearsal, including Claire and Charlotte, who Lola had begun calling the "wedding sisters," as Charlotte was a wedding planner and Claire always did the flowers. Tommy had a couple of sailing buddies all lined up, waiting for the rehearsal to begin. Among them was not Stan Ellis, the man Anna had had an affair with all those years ago— the man who'd ultimately made the mistake that had caused Anna to lose her life out on that boat.

Good, Lola thought to herself selfishly. *I don't want him here.*

Forgiveness was a beautiful thing. Lola could describe the benefits of it to herself time and time again, saying that it opened her mind and her heart and her soul to other possibilities and worlds. But she knew, in another way, she would never truly forgive Stan Ellis for what he'd done.

Her father had already arrived and stood off to the left of the church with Scott, Zach, and Tommy. Lola hugged her father lovingly, dipping her nose into the soft fabric of his button-down.

"There she is," Wes breathed. "The most beautiful bride on Martha's Vineyard."

"Oh goodness. Don't you compliment her too much. It'll go to her head," Zach teased.

"Good to see you too, smartypants," Lola quipped, sticking out her tongue playfully.

"The bride is such a lady," Tommy said, dropping forward to kiss her on the cheek.

Just before the pastor arrived to start the rehearsal, a car crept up the driveway to Grange Hall and parked in the back lot. Lola hadn't recognized the vehicle and stood, poised at the back pew, watching as Jenny and a handsome stranger, presumably her boyfriend, stepped up the staircase and entered. Lola's heart lifted at the sight of Jenny, her previous family, and a woman she'd thought might slightly detest her, especially after the strange meeting up in Boston.

But Jenny had never been resentful. Lola wrapped

her arms around her lovingly and closed her eyes as she whispered, "Thank you for being here today. I only wish that Valerie would make the trip here from, ha, Oak Bluffs."

Jenny leaned back, her smile crooked and sad. "She's so close yet so far."

Lola shrugged. "All that matters is that you're here."

"I don't know. I think it matters that we're together again. Especially to celebrate such a big event in your life," Jenny offered.

Lola's heart thumped strangely as she stepped back from the hug. The pastor had arrived and instructed everyone to set up in their locations: Audrey, Susan, Amanda, and Christine in the back of the church, along with two of Tommy's dear friends. Grandpa Wes barrelled back into the foyer as well, prepared to take his youngest daughter down the aisle.

"You're reading the poem I sent you?" Lola asked Jenny distractedly as she headed back to the foyer.

"I have it right here," Jenny confirmed, tapping her purse.

"Thank you. Thank you so much."

Lola rushed back to the foyer, where she found her sisters, her niece, her daughter, her father, and Tommy's dearest friends, all in bubbly conversation about who would win the Round-the-Island Sailing Race that year.

"Tommy's always a shoo-in," Amanda pointed out.

"Yeah, but that Cole Steel ain't half bad," Grandpa Wes returned.

"He did look fantastic last year," Susan stated. "But I still think Tommy's got it. Especially this year, hot off the heels of his wedding." She elbowed Lola and smiled.

"Is everyone ready?" The pastor waved a hand from

the front of Grange Hall, his eyes alight. "We're going to get the music started in five, four, three, two..."

Chapter Seventeen

Lola spent the night at the Sheridan House, sleeping beside her daughter and having delirious dreams about the future and the past, all mixed. In one, she and Tommy were twenty-five years old with a little toddler boy who celebrated a birthday with a brand-new toy tricycle. In another, Audrey was an old woman coaxing Lola to eat a big bowl of potato soup. In another, Anna Sheridan carried Stan Ellis's boat on her shoulders like a strongman in a circus— her eyes alight, as though she did that sort of thing all the time.

When Lola awoke, it was six thirty in the morning. She would marry Tommy Gasbarro at four thirty that afternoon, which seemed like a lifetime away. Beside her in bed, Audrey continued to sleep, her thumb a few inches from her mouth, acting as a reminder that, no matter how old and big she got, she would always be that little girl whose thumb-sucking addiction nearly ruined her first-grade experience.

Recently, Max had moved to the bedroom next door in the Sheridan House, which was both heartening and saddening at once. The past three times that Lola had slept over, Max hadn't woken up in the middle of the night even once. It was the end of an era.

Lola made her way downstairs, brewed a pot of coffee, and sat at the kitchen table, forcing herself to breathe deeply. Midway through her meditation, Amanda stepped out of her bedroom and nearly leaped with surprise.

"It's the bride!" she murmured, making sure she wasn't too loud to wake the rest of the house.

Amanda was dressed in a sports bra and a pair of tight shorts. "I'm going to do a yoga video," she explained. "Any chance you'd like to join me?"

But Lola's thoughts swirled too quickly for something as stable and solid as yoga. Instead, she insisted she'd gotten up early to do something she hadn't done in literally years: go running. As she tied up her dusty tennis shoes and trounced out the door, she half regretted her decision. By the time she stretched her legs out toward the road, getting into a firm jog, she fully regretted it. *I can't turn back now. Amanda would force me into yoga. And besides. Don't I want to feel empowered on my wedding day? Don't I want to feel strong and alive and open to the possibilities of life?*

Lola began to run out toward the Sunrise Cove Inn, grateful that each stride made her legs scream less than the one before. As she ran past the inn itself, she waved a hand to Sam as he opened the back shed, a confident smile on his face.

"See you later, Sam!" Lola hollered as she passed, which caused him to say something she couldn't exactly hear in return.

She continued along Pall Mall Street, down Dudley

Avenue, all the way to Simpson Avenue, where she dropped down and gripped her knees, seizing with adrenaline and fatigue. When she rose to check her phone, she read a message from none other than Jenny.

> JENNY: Happy wedding day, beautiful.
>
> JENNY: I reached out to Valerie last night. No answer. And actually, it went straight to voicemail.
>
> JENNY: Feeling strange and nervous about it. I feel like, no matter how angry Valerie is with you, she's still happy for you in her own way.
>
> JENNY: I just thought she would have reached out by now, is all.

Lola tilted her head as she read and reread the messages, her heart pumping. She quickly searched again for Harry Billson's address, realizing she was little more than a ten-minute run away. Did she dare head over there and bang down the door mere hours before her wedding?

Then again— didn't she want Valerie at her wedding? Didn't she want the air to clear before she fully stepped forward into her new life?

Lola sprinted toward Harry Billson's place, her legs screaming throughout and her hair stretching wildly behind her. Somewhere along the way, she'd lost her hair tie, which gave her a Disney's *Pocahontas* look— one she would have coveted as a much younger girl.

The stretch of fence she'd seen on the satellite image appeared off to the left, about a quarter mile from where she had to stop running. She staggered toward it, trying to calm her breath, and found that the fence wrapped around the entire property. When she reached the edge, she leaped up to peer over it but couldn't see anything but the tiptops of trash piles.

Trash piles?

This was such a contrast to the Valerie that Lola had met all those years ago, the coolest woman in the world and someone Lola felt honored to call her friend.

Oh, Valerie. If you're here, why did you stay? This isn't your world. You deserve so much more.

The online photographs showed a fence without an opening. Fortunately for Lola's mission, however, someone had recently yanked the fence open at the entry of the driveway. Lola found herself in the gap between the street and Harry's private property, her heart pounding. She'd listened to one too many true-crime podcasts not to believe what she was doing was completely safe.

Up ahead, the garage door was open to reveal a garage fit for a hoarder. Garbage bags and newspapers lined the big room, where a large Rottweiler sat panting in the middle. Across the property, the trash heaps lifted into the sky alongside clunky-looking vehicles, some of which were rusted out. Others were gleaming and looked expensive, as though they'd been taken right from the pages of a magazine.

Every single alarm bell in Lola's head rang out at once.

And then, on cue, came yelling from inside the house.

"You're always going on and on about that. Don't you ever get the hint that you should shut your mouth?"

The masculine and charged voice sent shivers up and down Lola's spine. *What kind of man speaks to a woman like that? A man who hates himself and is willing to bring the world down along with him,* she thought.

Lola lifted her chin and charged toward the garage, inhaling the smell of rotten food. Wrinkling her nose, she paused at the edge of the garage, eyeing a strange oil stain in the very center, directly next to the now-growling dog.

Within, the horrible voice grew louder. "I shouldn't have ever given you an inch. Everyone knows that when you give a woman like you an inch, they take a mile."

The Rottweiler's teeth were fully bared as he started to growl. Lola extended her palms out flatly as she whispered, "Shhh. No reason to freak out, bud. We're all in this together."

But the Rottweiler jumped up to all fours and raised his chin. Lola's eyes flashed toward the door between the garage and the rest of the house. The doorknob was stained with a thousand grubby fingerprints.

Should I just run in there? Open the door? Demand that Valerie comes with me?

It was unrealistic to think that way, wasn't it? Couples fought. Probably, if someone had listened in on one of her rows with Tommy, they'd have charged into their cabin, as well.

In the righthand corner, a large stack of metal glinted. The metal was in multiple colors—blue, red, green, and yellow—and each piece seemed bent out and rusted. Lola stepped toward them tentatively and leaned down to inspect them.

With a strange surge in her heart, she realized that these metal slabs were old license plates, clearly removed from vehicles.

"Just stop your crying, will you?" The voice rang out from the main house.

Lola shivered and returned her gaze to the stack of

license plates. The one on the very top was blue from the state of Massachusetts. The license plate read DTXQ12.

"DTXQ12," Lola muttered to herself, reaching forward to remove the top plate so she could read the next one. But as she began to fold the first one upward, like turning the page of a book, the Rottweiler began to howl longingly. Lola turned around and panicked, allowing the license plates to fall back in place. Lola managed to leap away from the stack of license plates just in the nick of time.

Immediately, the door between the main house and the garage burst open to reveal Harry Billson, a handsome man in his midthirties with a propensity for thick mustaches, dark-blue baseball caps, and jeans with flashes of car oil stains across them. He gaped at her, this stranger in his garage, and his eyes glinted menacingly.

How would she get out of this?

"Harry!" Lola began brightly, overacting the part of an eager and friendly woman. "Harry, I'm so sorry to barge in on you like this."

Harry cocked his left eyebrow high and tilted his head. In a sense, he reminded Lola of the Rottweiler, as both seemed eager to tear her apart.

"I've never seen you before in my life," Harry shot back.

Lola tried to peer behind Harry to spot some sign of Valerie.

"I'm really good friends with Valerie," she stuttered. "The best of friends. We've had a few struggles lately. We've fought. And I really regret that."

Harry continued to gape at her with sizzling confusion.

"But today is my wedding day. And I don't know if I

can marry my fiancé without Valerie there to support me," Lola continued hurriedly. "If you could just let me speak with her for a moment."

"A wedding?" Harry sniffed. "I've never heard of any wedding." He yanked his head back to peer down the hallway, proof that Valerie was the woman he'd just been ripping into. "Valerie? There's someone here to see you."

"Who is it?" Valerie's voice was sharp-edged and entirely unlike the version of Valerie Lola had known for years.

"Some woman who says she's your best friend." Harry gave Lola a sneaky smile, one that seemed to suggest that already, he had "won" Valerie. She wouldn't be coming back from the prison he'd built her.

Finally, Valerie appeared at the far end of the white-washed hallway. Lola could only make out one-half of her face and the strands of her glossy hair. Their eyes connected for a split second before Harry burst into laughter.

"But I should tell her what I already know, shouldn't I?" Harry continued. "That anyone who crosses you is out for good. You've had your fights? That means she's already shown you everything you need to know about herself. Case closed. Right, Valerie?"

Lola's throat tightened. "If we could just talk for five minutes, Valerie. Please..."

"I think I'm going to need to ask you to leave my property," Harry shot back. "Immediately."

Harry then slammed the door between them, leaving Lola in a quivering state of shock. She glanced back at the license plates, at the oil stain, and at the growling Rottweiler, her heart heavy as a stone. She then darted around and raced off the property, all the way back to the

Sheridan House, feeling as though a monster followed her the entire way. When she returned to the house, she texted Valerie.

LOLA: If you want to get out of there, just say the word.

LOLA: I'm ready to pick you up whenever.

LOLA: I'll drive over in my wedding dress if I have to.

But to this, Valerie only texted:

VALERIE: We're living different lives now.

VALERIE: We don't need each other.

VALERIE: I certainly don't need you.

Chapter Eighteen

Amanda sat on the back porch of the Sheridan House with little Mia in her arms, watching the waves as they coursed along the private beach, glittering with the promise of a brand-new day. Mia slept beautifully, her eyes tilting left and right beneath her eyelids and her right hand in a fist. At nearly six months old, Mia had become very animated lately, babbling nondescript words and presenting a personality that was quite different from Max's yet addictive for all members of the Sheridan clan. To Amanda, who found herself craving babies of her own more and more, she treasured these moments alone with Mia. It allowed her to peer into the future and see herself doing just this, her heart enormous with love for her own child.

Would it be Sam's child? Only time would tell.

Down below along the beach, Lola burst forth in running gear. She flung her tennis shoes back along the sand and stepped into the waves, her chin lifted toward the horizon. Amanda had never in her life seen Lola exercise on purpose, and the sight was as captivating as it was alarming. What had gotten into her?

Susan stepped out of the kitchen area with a mug of coffee lifted. "What's gotten into Lola?"

"I saw her this morning when I woke up to do yoga," Amanda offered. "But that was over an hour ago. Has she been running this whole time?"

"Maybe this is the married version of Lola," Susan quipped. "Next thing we know, she'll be asking us to make her green smoothies and meditate with her on the beach."

"Likely," Amanda offered sarcastically.

"Who wants a mimosa?" Christine called from the kitchen, where she'd begun to brew up supplies for their wedding preparation schedule. Everyone knew that weddings were better when they glittered with mimosas.

"The hairstylists will be here in about twenty minutes," Susan offered. "Lola needs to shower, like ASAP."

Down below, Lola grabbed her tennis shoes and sprang up the hill between the beach and the Sheridan House. When she reached the base of the porch, she lifted her eyes toward Susan and Amanda. Something about her was off, something Amanda couldn't fully place. Was she having doubts about her wedding? Was this what Chris had gone through hours before he'd bailed on Amanda at the altar?

"Did I hear mimosas?" Lola said finally, forcing a smile.

"You did." Christine stepped out with a glowing orange glass and a strawberry stabbed across the side. "First one's for the bride, of course."

Lola hustled up the steps for the mimosa. Her legs shone with sweat.

"Have you been running?" Christine demanded doubtfully. "Audrey couldn't figure out where you'd gone."

"Mom. Are you sick? Maybe her nerves have taken over?" Audrey called from within, where she fed Max with a purple plastic spoon.

Lola laughed good-naturedly and sipped the mimosa, her eyes closed. There was a shock wave around her, as though nobody could reach out and touch her. After she sipped, she stepped into the shadows of the Sheridan House to greet Audrey and Max, leaving Christine, Amanda, Susan, and Mia on the porch. Christine arched her brow with confusion.

"What happened?" Susan mouthed.

But very soon after Lola's return from her strange run, time forced them forward. The three hairstylists they'd hired arrived and set to work on Audrey, Amanda, and Christine while Susan watched Max and kept tabs on Mia. Lola returned from her shower a little while later, sheepish but mostly back to normal. Audrey demanded that they play music and came up with silly conversation topics, things like:

"If you could marry any celebrity in the world, who would it be?"

And "if money wasn't a problem, who would you get to design your wedding dress?"

And "Susan, which wedding did you like the most? The one to Richard, or the one to Scott?"

To this, Susan blushed and glanced toward the ground. "I think I knew, in my heart of hearts, that Richard wasn't 'the one' for me. But gosh, that wedding was a blast. Both of my children had already been born, and if I remember correctly, Jake revealed himself to be one heck of a dancer at that wedding. Everyone ate up his skills."

"He and Kristen are still coming, aren't they?" Lola asked.

"They got here last night," Susan affirmed. "I stopped by the Sunrise Cove Inn on my way back from the rehearsal dinner to say hello. The twins were out like a light, so I have to play catch-up on my grandma time today and tomorrow. Unfortunately, Jake and Kristen need to get back to Newark by Monday."

"They should really come and spend some real time here on the Vineyard," Amanda offered. "They'd love it."

"I mentioned I could take the twins for a week or two this summer, as well," Susan said. "While Jake and Kristen go on some sort of vacation together. God knows they need it after the hell they went through during the early days of having the twins."

"One at a time is enough," Christine murmured, glancing over at Mia's sleep monitor.

"I think they've blocked out the majority of the painful memories at this point," Susan said with a laugh.

"Still can't believe you wanted to move in with them after the divorce," Amanda chided. "Can you imagine where your life would be? You'd be knitting little sweaters, making iced tea, and gossiping about the neighbors."

"I'd still like a knitted sweater, Susie," Lola joked. "No matter how many criminal cases you take this year. Get ready to knit!"

Susan laughed as she stretched her hand over her newly curled updo. Amanda's heart surged with love for her mother, her favorite person in the world— the woman she most wanted to become when she was younger. She'd watched her overcome so much throughout her forties.

What awaits me as I get older?

Cancer? Divorce? Sorrow? Loss?

Will I handle it with as much grace as Susan Sheridan?

Suddenly, Amanda heard herself ask something she'd never imagined she'd have enough strength to ask.

"What did you think of me when Chris left me at the altar?"

There was a strange moment of silence, during which the Sheridan clan eyed Amanda curiously, just as confused as she was that the question had come out.

"Someone left you at the altar, honey?" one of the hairstylists asked.

"Men can be so all over the place," the other cooed. "You never know what they're thinking because they don't even know what they're thinking. No self-reflection. No communication!"

"To be honest with you," Audrey began, "I never liked the guy."

Amanda laughed inwardly. Audrey had said the sentiment many times, but each time seemed lighter and less judgmental.

"I just really wanted to get married," Amanda explained to the hairstylists.

"That can happen," one of them offered. "I see it all the time in this line of work. Women feel this ticking clock and just flail around and pick the guy who's closest to them."

"I can tell you that I never did that," Lola affirmed.

"Honey, that's clear. Nobody has to get married once

they hit forty," another stylist joked. "Once you're forty, you do it because you're actually in love, I think. That's my current theory, anyway."

"I'd back up that theory," another told them.

Susan crossed and uncrossed her eyes as confusion played out across her face. "I guess I'm the only one here who really saw your relationship with Chris up close."

Amanda's heart seized with a thousand little memories: the first time Chris had met Susan and worn a bright pink tie; the first time Susan had baked Chris a platter of cookies before his midterm; the time Chris and Amanda had picked Susan up from the airport, just a week or so after Richard's affair with Penelope had come out.

"Amanda, you loved him. For a little while, I believe that you really loved him and he really loved you. But sometimes, unfortunately, and for reasons none of us can fully understand, love doesn't last," Susan said finally.

"Ain't it the truth," one of the hairstylists said.

Amanda nodded, dropping her eyes to the ground.

"But that doesn't mean you shouldn't allow yourself to try again," Christine said knowingly, as though she could already feel the "meaning" behind Amanda's question.

"And I think I know a gentleman who seems more than willing to try again with you," Susan said, her eyes twinkling.

Upstairs, baby Mia cried out as she erupted from sleep. Amanda laughed as the cry seemed a direct link to her emotions. Somehow, we all must wake up to a brand-new day, get accustomed to our new surroundings, and continue to try, try again.

Chapter Nineteen

Lola sat in the back of the rented limousine in her bohemian wedding dress, with its ivory lace across the hands and the flowing skirt. Flowers adorned her dark curls, and she wore light-blue pointed shoes, slightly heeled, which played in such a contrast to her "normal" bohemian boots. Beside her, Audrey sat in an emerald gown, her eyes upon Lola as they shared the pre-wedding silence.

"You know, you give me the word? I'll leap in the front seat of this limousine and drive us out of here," Audrey joked.

Lola, whose head was heavy with confusion, gave Audrey a wry smile. After a deep breath, she shoved thoughts of Valerie and Harry deep into the back alleys of her mind and gave herself a pep talk: *Two hundred and forty-seven guests have gathered here today to celebrate my wedding to the love of your life. I'm not going to taint this because some idiot said a few harsh words to you in his disgusting garage.*

"You good?" Audrey's smile faltered as she laced her fingers through Lola's.

Lola tilted her head as her heart swelled with memories. "You know after your father left..."

"Uh-oh. Mom's getting nostalgic," Audrey teased.

"Just let me talk. It's my wedding day, isn't it?"

"All right. Go for it." Audrey tossed her hair across her shoulder like a dark curtain.

"After your father left, I was so sure that nobody would be good enough for us," Lola continued. "We sat in the kitchen, sang songs, made up little dances, and made jokes about boys being icky."

Audrey laughed. "They still are, right?"

"Absolutely," Lola affirmed. "Yesterday, I caught Tommy eating a four-day-old chicken wing from the paper bag in the back of the fridge. But I digress. The fact is, for all those years, it was just you and me. And now, we have the entire Sheridan clan, plus some men who aren't half bad."

"Not half bad at all," Audrey offered back.

Suddenly, a hand rapped at the window above Audrey's head. There, Susan Sheridan called that it was time for them to collect themselves at the back of Grange Hall in preparation for the ceremony. Lola drew her shoulders back as she whispered, "It's showtime."

June 18th, Lola Sheridan's wedding day, had morphed into a gloriously blissful, near-summer day of seventy-four degrees with a glossy blue sky above and blossoming trees that swelled and flashed their leaves with the slight breeze. For a moment before entering Grange Hall, Lola lifted her chin and closed her eyes, acknowledging the weight of so many, many decades of loneliness. It was in the past, now.

Her father stood, nervous and pale, at the doorway between the foyer and the grand hall in which the ceremony would take place. He scuffed his expensive shoes and muttered to himself, his dark hair catching the light from the on-high chandelier.

"Dad. The bride's here!" Christine announced brightly, placing a hand on their father's shoulder adoringly.

Wes lifted his chin to find Lola as she stepped through the double-wide doors, her skirts lifted gently to allow her blue shoes to shine forth. Their eyes connected for a long moment as Wes's chin wiggled, threatening tears.

"You look beautiful, Lola," Wes whispered finally, drawing his hand forward.

Lola's smaller hand found his, and together, they stepped toward the rest of the bridesmaids, their smiles lengthening. The pianist in the grand hall had begun to play the entrance music, which would bring the bridesmaids down the aisle to make way for the bride. This was "Pachelbel's Canon," a classic favorite and one that seemed appropriately sophisticated to Lola. When Lola had asked Tommy's opinion about the song, he'd shrugged and said, "If it isn't a song from the oldies station, then I'm not sure what it is. Sounds fine to me." Lola had laughed outrageously at that, grateful for Tommy's sense of humor and his overwhelming ability to make her weak at the knees.

"It's showtime," Wes muttered to the rest of the Sheridan women, stepping back as the first of them began to walk down the aisle. First came Amanda, followed by Susan, followed by Christine, with Audrey in the very back.

Just before she began her trek down, Audrey reached back and gripped Lola's hand. Her eyes said everything Lola already felt. *I can't believe we've made it this far together. Our story isn't done, not by a long shot.*

As "Pachelbel's Canon" finished out, drawing the bridesmaids along one end of the hall and the grooms along the other, the song shifted toward the song Lola had decided upon to walk down: "This Year" by The Zombies, a piano version.

Right before they took a step forward together, Wes leaned toward Lola and whispered, "Your mother would be so proud of you. I hope you know that."

Lola's throat tightened as tears threatened to fall.

"And not just for falling in love, either," Wes added. "For going after your dreams. For not letting any pitfall get in your way. And for that enormous heart of yours, which seems to contain enough emotion for a thousand stories. I'm lucky to have you as my daughter, Lola. I really am."

Charlotte, the wedding planner, hustled across the back of Grange Hall to mutter, "Lola! It's time."

Lola and Wes then locked eyes, nodded, counted silently in time, and then stepped out into the aisle, headed for the pastor at the far end, there between the groomsmen and the bridesmaids. As she walked, Tommy stepped out from behind the groomsmen to take his rightful place there in the center, his chest puffed out and his hands crossed in front of him. His Italian leather shoes caught the sunlight that glittered in through the windows, and his thick black hair was styled to perfection into small waves that cascaded toward his ears. His black eyes told a story of intelligence, intrigue, and a sense of adventure. As Lola walked toward him, with all eyes upon her, her stomach stirred with the depth of her truth: this was the only man for her.

At the far end of the aisle, Tommy and Wes shook hands before Wes turned back to sit in the first pew next to Aunt Willa, who'd appeared in their lives the previous December and left a real mark, illuminating information about Anna Sheridan that the Sheridan women had never known. Aunt Willa gave a little excited wave and then gripped Wes's hand knowingly. On the other end of Grange Hall, located on Tommy's side, was Aunt Beatrice, who, when Lola glanced over at her, seemed to stare directly at Wes rather than the bride and groom.

Lola's stomach twisted with laughter. When she turned back to find Tommy before her, all dressed in his tuxedo and wearing a stern expression, her smile faltered all over again. This was really happening. This was her wedding day, one of the biggest moments of her life. She wanted to memorize every single detail.

"Good afternoon, ladies and gentlemen," the pastor began, his voice endearing as it found traction. "Today, we celebrate the union of two of the most free-spirited creatures I've ever had the pleasure of meeting. When I sat in conversation with both of them privately, they each told me that they never imagined themselves settling down, not for anyone or any reason. The fact that we're here today is proof in point that people need people— that love conquers even the most aimless soul— and that there really is such a thing as soul mates."

Lola and Tommy locked eyes for a long moment as the pastor continued, peppering in personal details about a mostly traditional service. Halfway through the service, Jenny stood to read a poem:

"You and I

155

Have so much love,
That it
Burns like a fire,
In which we bake a lump of clay
Molded into a figure of you
And a figure of me.
Then we take both of them,
And break them into pieces,
And mix the pieces with water,
And mold again a figure of you,
And a figure of me.
I am in your clay.
In life, we share a single quilt.
In death, we will share a single coffin."

Kuan Tao-Sheng, one of the first beloved female painters and poets in Chinese history, wrote the poem. She'd lived between the 1200s and 1300s and, for a brief time, had been considered the "second" wife of a renowned male painter. After reading this poem, entitled "Married Love," he'd only decided to remain faithful to Kuan, knowing no other wife but her. The story of Kuan Tao-Sheng had illuminated Lola, Valerie, and Jenny's lives back in Boston when they'd been scrappy artists and poets in their own right. It felt fitting that Jenny had selected this poem. The words filled Lola's eyes with tears.

"Both Lola and Tommy have written their own vows for this service," the pastor continued later. "Which shouldn't come as a surprise to anyone, given their individualized natures."

Lola began with her vows, which she'd written over a number of months, editing and rewriting and ultimately throwing out three different versions.

"Tommy. Nearly two years ago, I approached you with an idea for an article about your sailing prowess. I pitched it to you as 'A write-up on the most courageous sailor on the seven seas.' Throughout that initial conversation, I quivered with fear. Maybe something within me understood that you were it for me. Maybe something within me understood that everything in my life would change forever when I got on that boat. As many of our friends and family know, a storm ripped across the seas that weekend, terrifying me to a degree that I found difficult to describe with words. Me, a writer."

At this, the crowd chuckled good-naturedly.

"But your strong and capable body and know-how out across the open sea brought us back to clear waters. And after the storm lifted and we sat again, watching the sunset, I thought to myself, 'I never want anything else but this.'" Lola heaved a sigh and swallowed the lump in her throat, grateful that she'd still been able to keep the tears at bay. "Thank you, Tommy, for helping me ride out the storm of this life. Thank you for wrapping me up in your strong arms, for knowing me and loving me for the wild woman I am. May we always be adventurous. May we always have hope. And may we always have the sea. I love you."

Lola then slid Tommy's wedding ring over his fourth finger, making it jump over his knuckle. This was it.

"I don't know how to follow that," Tommy joked, taking the microphone.

The crowd laughed again. When Lola glanced over at them, there wasn't a dry eye in sight.

"As many of you know, I'm not the writer here. The vows I've written are clunky and not poetic. They're probably filled with grammatical errors and misspellings.

But before I get started, I have to say my vows are totally from the heart. No doubt about that," Tommy continued.

"Lola. You're the most creative, intelligent, open-minded, and adventurous woman I've ever met. For years, I never thought I wanted a partner by my side until I met you, the only woman I've ever known who not only keeps up with me but seems to run circles around me. I look forward to many more decades of wild adventures, long afternoons on the beach, late nights of whiskey and conversation, and, naturally, barbecues at the Sheridan House. I've never been included in such a tight-knit family, but I knew, with the engagement to you, that I was latching myself to a large clan of loud, funny, and good-hearted people. I'm pleased to say that from today on, they're not only just like family. They actually are."

Tommy blinked back tears and glanced toward his side of Grange Hall, where Beatrice sat in the first pew. Lola could practically feel his heartbreaking all over again at the space where his mother should have sat.

"I love you, Lola. And I always will," Tommy finished before passing the microphone back to the pastor. He then slid the ring over Lola's finger, a symbol that paired them together for the rest of their days. It glinted beautifully around her fourth finger, adding a weight that Lola had never imagined.

A married woman. Me?

Yet it feels so right.

Chapter Twenty

That evening's sunset glowed with pastel pinks and lavenders, stretching out across the Vineyard sky and echoing across the clouds. The exterior of Grange Hall had been decorated blissfully with a summer garden feel, with twinkling lights that stretched around the dance floor, a long white table filled with food and drink, and a number of round tables with glowing white tablecloths. Immediately after dinner, the ten-piece band began to play big-band hits like "Sing, Sing, Sing," which brought Amanda to her feet, tugging Sam along with her.

"We have to go," she whispered. "Come on!"

Out on the dance floor, Sam placed his hand at the base of Amanda's back and swung her around in time, never missing a step. Amanda's hair flashed around her as they went, becoming the main focus on the dance floor. Audrey howled from a nearby table, saying, "That's my cousin! That's my girl!" and Amanda laughed, bubbling from champagne and the splendor of the evening.

When the song finished, she and Sam collapsed in

one another's arms as a small crowd applauded. Amanda breathed into Sam's shoulder, "I had no idea what a good dancer you were."

To this, Sam said, "You never asked."

From the side of the dance floor, Amanda watched as Grandpa Wes stepped toward Beatrice, bent down to whisper in her ear, and then extended his hand. Amanda jabbed Sam in the stomach to get his attention.

"They're at it again," she whispered.

"It's the reality TV show all over again!" Sam cried. "*Lovewatching*."

"That's still a temporary title," Amanda teased.

Beatrice and Grandpa Wes stepped into the center of the dance floor, with Beatrice lifting her chin to speak to Wes as they eased from side to side. This particular song was slower, allowing them to flirt and laugh easily without getting out of breath.

"They seem so happy," Sam whispered. "I hope that I can feel that happy when I'm that age."

"I think it's a choice," Amanda offered. "Something you have to wake up every day and decide on. At least, that's what I've decided the past year and a half since I officially moved to the Vineyard."

Sam lowered his head and kissed her cheek lovingly, his hand stretching across the flat of her stomach. *Does he think about having children with me? Does he imagine our future?*

"It's time to cut the cake!" Audrey hollered out a few minutes later, curling Amanda's hair around her finger as she bobbed Max toward the multitiered cake.

Amanda and Sam held hands and headed for the corner, where, beneath the growing darkness of the night, Tommy and Lola sliced the cake together with a single knife and then placed little morsels of cake on top of one another's tongues. Shoving cake into mouths wasn't exactly the Lola and Tommy way.

After the cake was cut, Sam grabbed his and Amanda's two plates and returned to the table, where Amanda sat with Noah, Max, and Audrey. Max looked wide-eyed and sleepy, and Audrey admitted that she'd have to put him to bed shortly. Noah lifted him into his arms and turned in circles until Max howled with laughter. Audrey rose up on her toes and kissed them both, first Max and then Noah. Beneath the table, Sam held Amanda's hand delicately as her throat tightened.

"How does it feel to have Lola married off?" Amanda asked Audrey when she returned to her seat to tear through her cake.

Audrey placed a large slab of mostly icing on her tongue. Amanda adored this about her cousin: the fact that she ate dessert first, that icing was her favorite food group, and that she often laughed until she cried.

"I half-expected both of them to run in opposite directions when they got to the front of the Hall," Audrey joked. "Maybe they both had a getaway car waiting in the parking lot."

"No, but seriously. It must feel strange," Amanda continued to probe.

Audrey licked a small piece of icing from her lower lip. "I thought it would feel like this big door slamming between the past and the future. Like, there's a before and an after, and now, we're in the after. But actually, it doesn't feel that way at all." Audrey's eyes glittered knowingly. "Although if you ever leave the Sheridan House, that's when I'll really cry."

Amanda's eyes widened. She hadn't actually considered what would happen to Audrey when Amanda finally moved out of the Sheridan House.

"Gosh. Moving in there was kind of an accident, wasn't it?" Amanda breathed.

"A happy accident that I refuse to give up," Audrey shot back. She then turned toward Noah and Sam and said, "What if we all live together in one big house? Huh?"

"Now, that's a reality TV show," Sam quipped.

"Oh, sure. We could do that," Audrey said. "We'll have to be more dramatic, though. Noah, what did you say you were mad at me about recently?"

Noah furrowed his brow. "Hmm. Wasn't it you, um, who played music too loudly at my house?"

"Not dramatic enough," Audrey affirmed. "We have to think bigger."

As the foursome laughed wildly, the bride appeared before them, grinning at Amanda and Audrey.

"I see you've eaten all the icing off your cake, honey," Lola teased. "You're my daughter, aren't you?"

"You're spot-on, Mom." Audrey jumped up to wrap her arms around her mother's waist. "Are you walking around demanding that everyone compliments you?"

"It's the only day you're legally allowed to do that," Amanda agreed.

Lola laughed and scanned across Amanda to Sam, who sat contemplatively, a forkful of cake lifted. After a dramatic pause, Lola's smile fell as she said something very strange.

"Sam. If I said the numbers DTXQ12 to you, what would you say in return?"

All the color drained from Sam's cheeks. He placed

the fork against the side of his plate and leaned forward. "Did you read that in the file?"

Lola closed her eyes as her shoulders drooped.

"Mom. What's going on?" Audrey demanded.

Lola stepped around Audrey and collapsed in the chair next to Amanda, speaking to both Amanda and Sam as her fingers toyed with the lace of her dress.

"You remember my friend, Valerie," she began. "Who was quite upset with me at my bachelorette party."

"Of course," Amanda affirmed.

"Well, she ended up with that guy on the island. The one she said she'd met. I wanted to reach out to her, tell her that I hated that we've drifted apart. But when I got to Harry's place, I found that it was totally trashed. Rusted cars in the yard. A scary Rottweiler in the garage. And a pile of license plates, including..."

"DTXQ12," Sam whispered, flabbergasted.

"You're kidding," Amanda gasped.

Lola shrugged. "I was totally blown away when I saw it. Harry was inside, screaming at Valerie, but when they discovered me, Valerie wouldn't come out. When I got home, it was full-scale wedding-wedding-wedding, and I didn't want anything to ruin the day. But I see you two, Sam and Amanda, plus Beatrice over there, still dancing with my father, and I think... This guy needs to be put away. Immediately."

Sam nodded firmly, his eyes alight. "You found him."

"I don't know. I don't know." Lola pressed the tips of her fingers across her forehead. "But if it is him..."

Sam erupted from his chair, reaching for his phone. "I'll take care of it, Lola. Get back to enjoying yourself."

Amanda stood with him, linking her fingers with his.

Lola nodded as she whispered, "I just hope and pray that Valerie isn't somehow involved in all this."

"She met him after the accident," Amanda remembered.

"Yes, but..." Lola trailed off for a moment. "Women do terrible things for men who manipulate them. My Valerie didn't have love for a long, long time. I just hope she's strong enough to step away."

Tommy appeared behind Lola, wrapping his arms around her. It was as though he'd sensed something was amiss. "What's going on, baby?"

"I think we might have found the man who caused the accident. He's a little too close to home," Lola breathed.

Chapter Twenty-One

Jenny and her boyfriend danced on the corner of the dance floor, both flushed with wine. Lola watched them from a distance, her heart bulging in her throat and her tongue sharply sweet from the cake.

"I'm just going to talk to Jenny really quick about this," she told Tommy. "And then, I promise, I'll let it all go."

Tommy nodded. "She was your best friend for a long, long time. I understand that you have to honor that."

Lola lifted up to kiss him again, wrapping her fingers around his and whispering, "I'm already so thankful that I married you!"

"Jenny." Lola appeared beside them, where Jenny's perfume wafted over her, crisp with something floral and vanilla.

"There she is. The woman of the hour." Jenny pressed her lips onto Lola's cheek.

"Thanks again for reading that poem," Lola said. "I remember being twenty-five? Twenty-six? And sitting with you and Val and thinking about this woman, Kuan Tao-Sheng, and the incredible power she exhibited with words. It was beyond my wildest dreams that I would ever have a love like Kuan did."

Jenny's eyes watered as she collected her boyfriend's hand in hers. "I feel the same."

Lola's ears thudded with the memory of that early morning, darting out from Harry's garage as Valerie crept around in the back of the house. Was that her happily ever after? Didn't she deserve so much more?

"I need to talk to you," Lola breathed.

Jenny's cheek twitched. "Let's not talk about her today, Lola. She's chosen her path. Today, we're celebrating yours."

"That isn't it." Lola pressed her tongue to the side of her cheek as she tugged Jenny toward the far end of the reception, where they stood near the wall of Grange Hall. There, Jenny crossed and uncrossed her arms distractedly, glancing back at her boyfriend as he refilled his cocktail.

"I went to see Valerie this morning. She didn't look like herself."

Jenny shrugged. "I think she said the same thing about you."

Lola's stomach twisted. "This is different, Jen. Really. Something is wrong with that guy. Now, we're pretty sure he was involved in the hit-and-run accident that totaled my niece's boyfriend's car and really injured Tommy's great-aunt."

Jenny furrowed her brow. "That guy? From the bar? You're sure?"

"No. I'm not really sure about anything. I just—" Lola

cleared her throat. "I feel terrible about the fact that we're all so distant from one another now. And..."

"And maybe you're projecting?" Jenny interjected. "Not to be rude. As I said, I want to celebrate with you today. You and Tommy and your union. Let's not talk about her. Please."

"I just..."

As Lola's eyes swirled around distractedly, she glanced over the surrounding twinkling lights toward the parking lot, where the shadow of a woman lurked, carrying a large wrapped present. Lola's heart seized as she leaped back, nearly toppling over the small heel of her blue shoe.

"Val?" she called out.

The woman wore a black dress with a dramatic V-neck and a flowing skirt, which the wind cut through dramatically, whipping it back behind her. When she drew closer, it was clear she'd been crying, and her cheeks were blotchy and slightly purple. As ever, her makeup was perfect (except for the soft stains from her crying), and her legs were muscular and gorgeous as they strung out from the skirt.

When Valerie reached them, she pressed the present toward Lola and dropped her eyes to the ground. Lola accepted the gift, genuinely surprised. It was almost like living out a dream.

"What are you doing here?" she asked Valerie.

Valerie shrugged. "I was invited, wasn't I?"

Jenny and Lola locked eyes for a moment.

"Yes. Of course, you were. I wanted you here so badly," Lola whispered, recognizing that she couldn't immediately demand what was going on. "It's just that I'm surprised."

Valerie ignored her. Instead, she glanced out across the gorgeous garden and its twinkling lights. "The moon hangs so perfectly over your party. Did you have to get a written permit to bring it here?"

Lola laughed, genuinely pleased with her joke. "Yeah. The process was a nightmare. God was like, 'You want to hire the moon on such short notice?'"

Valerie's beautiful eyes caught the twinkling lights. After another pause, she whispered, "I hope the ceremony went well?"

"Jenny read Kuan," Lola explained.

Valerie's eyes widened. "You're kidding. It's perfect."

"It really was," Lola agreed.

"We read that poem over and over again, amazed at that woman's power," Valerie breathed.

"We thought we were the most powerful women in the world," Lola affirmed. "And just because I got married doesn't mean I feel we've lost all that power. If you and Jenny and I could arrange more times to meet..."

Valerie lifted a hand and shook her head. "I was such a jerk that night at the cabin. I'm so sorry, Lola. When I saw you today outside of Harry's place, I felt jolted back to reality."

Lola placed her teeth on her lower lip. *Don't push her to admit he's insane. Don't shame her into this.*

"You don't know what it's like to feel like the world is going forward without you," Valerie breathed. "I suddenly was like, Oh my God. I'm forty. I haven't been in love in years, or maybe ever. And no man will ever care for me, not in any real way. When Harry asked me to come back to his place, he showered me with compliments and I love yous. It sounds so dumb to say aloud, but I finally felt special."

Lola's throat tightened. Already, she sensed where this story would go.

"As many women do, I shoved aside what I saw in front of me. Yes, there were heaps of trash around his yard. Yes, he had four rusted cars. Yes, he screamed at me sometimes, but only if he was grumpy when he woke up. Or drunk."

Lola shivered against the wall of the Grange Hall. Across from them, on the dance floor, her father remained latched tight with Beatrice, dancing slowly to ensure Beatrice's recently broken body remained okay.

"But Lola, when I saw you outside his place today, something broke inside me. I realized what a fool I've been. I saw you, and I remembered everything we've ever been through together. I remembered that there have been hard times and better times, and blissful times. I remembered that these times weren't necessarily based on the man I was kind of dating at the time. These times were based purely on what I built for myself. Or what we three built together."

"That's right," Jenny affirmed, dropping her eyes to the ground.

"Did you leave him?" Lola asked finally, her voice breaking.

Valerie nodded. "I did. He was so violent about it. He punched the wall with his fist. Blood everywhere..." Valerie lifted her hand to inspect her own skin as though she'd half imagined that his violence had lingered on her. "I grabbed my backpack and ran out the door, past the stupid trash bags and the newspapers and that dumb dog."

Jenny's eyes widened. "And you came directly here?"

Valerie shook her head. "I wasn't sure what to do, so I

eventually wound my way to the Sunrise Cove Inn. A woman named Natalie was working at the front desk. I told her my sob story and that I really needed to get to your wedding before it was too late. She lent me this dress and told me to bring this gift along with me."

Lola glanced at the tag on the present, which read: **TO: LOLA, LOVE: NATALIE.**

"So I'm sorry. I'm sorry that it's only me and my useless apology. All I can say is how sorry I am. And that I want to become friends again. And expunge that idiot Harry from my memories..."

Lola wasn't sure she wanted to add insult to injury. Instead, she fell forward, wrapping both Jenny and Valerie in a hug that seemed to transport them back to their early twenties. Back then, Audrey had been a toddler, and their free time had sizzled with pop music on the radio, bad snacks, and plenty of laughter.

When their hug broke, Lola leaned back and, finally, drummed up the courage to ask, "I don't suppose any of those cars in Harry's backyard was a Chevy Cavalier? A maroon one?"

Valerie's cheeks fell forward. "One of them, yeah. It was pretty messed up. It disappeared a little while ago, and I never figured out where it went. Harry was never one for questions. I finally just let it go."

Lola craned her head around to watch as Amanda and Sam, hand in hand, headed out for the parking lot. Her heart pounded knowingly. Soon, Sam would call the police and tell them what they now understood.

But there was no use getting Valerie more involved in that criminal's life.

"Why don't we dance? Like the old days?" Lola coaxed.

"God, remember that club we used to go to all the time?" Jenny said.

"We could only go if we got a babysitter for Audrey," Valerie said knowingly. "I remember it well."

"Well, lucky for us tonight, Audrey's twenty-one years old!" Lola joked, grabbing Valerie by her free hand. "I'll show you where that present goes. And then, let's head out there and dance the night away. For me. Okay?"

"Okay. I guess I will. For you," Valerie offered, her eyes twinkling.

Chapter Twenty-Two

Amanda hustled alongside Sam, watching as he dipped his hand into his pocket and drew out his phone. Behind them, Lola and Tommy's reception blared on without them, with big-band music ringing out across the hills and forests all the way to the coasts. It was difficult to imagine that anyone on the mainland could hear anything at all, which only added to the beauty of their party. The rest of the United States did their own thing while Martha's Vineyard partied in the east.

Just before Sam called them, he pressed his lips over Amanda's. Amanda stumbled back the slightest bit because of the passion of their kiss. When it broke, he blinked several times, coughed, then said, "Okay. Okay. Time to get this taken care of."

Amanda crossed her arms over her chest and listened as Sam spoke with the front desk manager of the police station, who, for once, wasn't the idiotic Connie. Sam described what they'd learned about the potential location of the license plate at one Harry Billson's place, located on the outskirts of Oak Bluffs.

"It's quite important to me that this is taken care of," Sam continued into the phone, his eyes dancing with the light from the reception. "My girlfriend and I were involved in the accident, as was an older woman. We could have been seriously injured. The fact that this hasn't been taken care of since the incident has kept me up at night."

Sam nodded as he listened to whatever it was the other person said. The words seemed to calm him. He finally brought his eyes toward Amanda's, and they illuminated with love and promise.

Did Chris ever look at me like that?

When Sam finally hung up the phone, he hugged Amanda warmly and said, "I think it'll be over soon."

"Thank goodness." Amanda shivered against him, overwhelmed with gratefulness and too many glasses of wine.

But before she knew what had happened, Sam's enormous form dropped down. He placed one knee forward and one leg back, and he lifted his hands to grip hers. All the air shot out from Amanda's lungs.

Is this really happening?

"Amanda Harris."

When Sam said Amanda's name, it was such an aphrodisiac. Amanda shivered, trying to memorize the sight of this handsome man down on one knee. *This is the last time this will ever happen. Don't miss it. Remember every moment.*

"When I met you a year and a half ago, I thought you were the most beautiful woman I'd ever seen," Sam began.

"That's—" Amanda began to protest, but Sam interrupted.

"Don't. Don't back away from this. I know you're scared. Heck, who wouldn't be? But Amanda, I love you. I love you with my whole heart and mind. You've taught me so much about myself and the way I want my life to go. Out there on the dance floor, I gazed down at you and realized that this was literally 'it' for me. I've never had that realization before."

Amanda's throat tightened. She longed to tell Sam that her engagement to Chris had been "just because it was time to get engaged." But she didn't want to taint this moment. She wanted to live in it, just the two of them, as long as it was capable of lasting.

"Will you, Amanda? Will you make me the happiest man on this island?" Sam continued. "We've already proven that we can handle everything, side-by-side. Why not this, too?"

Amanda pressed her lips together, overwhelmed with emotion. She then lifted her chin as her heart soared with happiness.

"I'll marry you, Sam Fuller. I can't imagine a better life."

Sam leaped up, wrapping his hands around the cinch of her waist and twirling her around and around. Amanda laughed until she pressed her lips against his, her heart pounding. When he finally, finally planted her back on the earth again, she kissed him again and then begged him, "You can't tell anyone about this!"

Sam's lips opened wide. "What are you talking about?"

Amanda laughed. "We can't ruin Lola's wedding with our own engagement. It's just rude!"

"Is this something only women know about?" Sam asked.

"Maybe," Amanda said. "I don't know. I just know that if we storm in there and tell everyone we got engaged, we'll get some strange looks. Let's just keep it our little secret for now. Okay?"

Sam shrugged, his smile still cartoonishly large. "Whatever you want, baby." He laced his fingers around her back and slow-danced with her for a long moment, there beneath the pregnant moon. It was terribly romantic, a moment that Amanda would return to throughout her life to remind herself of the density of real love.

When Sam and Amanda finally stepped back into the reception area, Audrey took one look at Amanda, dropped her jaw, and hissed, "You didn't."

Amanda tried to pretend she had no idea what Audrey spoke of. "What?"

"It's written all over your face," Audrey shot back. She grabbed Amanda's elbow knowingly and guided her toward their round table, where Noah sat with Beatrice, telling her about his love of the film *The Other Guys*, which Beatrice had obviously never seen.

"Tell me," Audrey demanded.

Amanda crossed and uncrossed her arms. "I don't know."

"What don't you know?"

"There's nothing to tell," Amanda tried.

Out on the dance floor, Sam spoke to Tommy good-naturedly, wearing a goofy grin.

"Look at him! He looks like he just jumped over the moon," Audrey said.

"He does not."

Audrey sighed. "You're being ridiculous. I would tell you if it happened to me."

Amanda's nostrils flared. "Still have no idea what you're saying."

"Oh. My. God." Audrey tossed her head back. "You're engaged. I know you're engaged. Just finally—"

But as she spat the words out, Amanda leaped forward and placed her hand over Audrey's mouth. "Will you shut your big mouth, Audrey!"

At this, Audrey howled knowingly and tossed her arms around Amanda. "I knew it," she breathed. "The minute you disappeared into the parking lot, I knew you'd come back an engaged woman. But dammit! That means you're leaving the Sheridan House, isn't it?"

"Let's not get ahead of ourselves," Amanda breathed, her heart surging with sorrow. "Let's just enjoy the night. Okay?"

Together, she and Audrey turned back to watch as Lola and Tommy kissed beneath the moonlight, their faces youthful and alive and their arms wrapped tenderly around one another. Sam soon joined their table with a fresh slice of cake and kissed Amanda delicately before flashing Audrey a look of disdain.

"You told her, didn't you?" he muttered to Amanda.

"What?" Amanda and Audrey cried in unison.

"I don't know anything," Audrey tried.

"Yeah. Right." And with that, Sam snapped his lips around another bite of cake, shaking his head with dismay. Only his eyes shone with humor.

Chapter Twenty-Three

Hit-and-Run Reveals Inner Workings of a Much Bigger Criminal Organization

Reported By: Audrey Sheridan

Last month, the island of Martha's Vineyard was rocked by a dramatic hit-and-run out on State Road. Given the neighborly instincts of most Vineyard residents, it seemed outside the bounds of reason to imagine that someone— the driver of a maroon Chevy Cavalier— could smash into a vehicle, causing a three-vehicle crash, and then U-turn into the road from whence he'd come and disappear.

The story grew even more strange afterward when two of the victims of the crash found the "runaway" vehicle along the edge of the water in Chilmark, thus allowing officers to conclude that whoever was guilty in the hit-and-run case wouldn't be easy to find.

Lola read the article aloud on the back porch of the Sheridan House, with Audrey, Amanda, Max, Christine, and Susan seated around the table alongside her. Two bottles of rosé cooled in ice buckets in the center. Upstairs, Max and Mia took their mid-afternoon naps, graciously allowing the Sheridan women a few hours of gossip time.

And, just in time, the *Martha's Vineyard Gazette* had arrived, hot off the presses, with the inclusion of Audrey's well-researched article.

"Dang, Audrey," Amanda breathed. "You're a real writer."

Audrey laughed. "The article is so long, Mom. You shouldn't read the whole thing."

"Come on. It's brilliant," Lola boasted proudly. "You tore into this big criminal gang and found out the inner workings of all the cars they were stealing on the East Coast. Harry was just a cog in their machine."

Audrey waved a hand knowingly, her eyes dancing. In truth, Lola had been terrified the past two weeks as Audrey had driven across Boston, interviewing police officers and other gang members who were willing to talk. Essentially, Harry's scrapyard had revealed a greater illegal community, which was the reason Harry had fled the scene of the hit-and-run in the first place. It seemed stranger than fiction, but it was real life. Plain and simple.

"I was glad that Valerie agreed to be interviewed," Audrey offered, placing a chip on her tongue and chewing slowly. "I know she's embarrassed that she ever got involved with that guy. But I just told her that Max is my greatest love— and he's the result of a very stupid affair I had out in Chicago."

"Are you suggesting that all women have done very stupid things for men?" Christine asked, feigning shock.

"I would never go that far," Audrey shot back sarcastically.

"What did she say in the article?" Amanda asked.

Lola scanned through to find Valerie's quotes, which discussed Harry's "strange habits" and his "even stranger friends." According to Valerie, Harry frequently left the house around midnight and could be heard having phone calls in the garage, during which he often yelled about "stuff he could hide" and "stuff he couldn't manage to hide."

"It was terrifying," Valerie told Audrey in the article. "Never knowing exactly what he was up to kept me up at night. I'd told this man I'd loved him— and I wasn't sure what he would do if I ever left him. He was a master manipulator. Hopefully, I've learned my lesson."

It was now the end of June. Sun-kissed waves crept toward the beach, cresting before they flashed across the sands. After Lola finished reading the last of the article, she led the rest of the Sheridan women to the beach, where they held hands and gazed out across the waters. Her heart swelled with a mix of sorrow and pride and joy.

"I can't believe you'll be gone for two weeks," Audrey breathed beside her, gripping her hand.

"Two weeks is nothing," Susan tried from the far end of their link. "Try twenty-five years. That's how long I went, basically, without talking to your mother. I'll never get those years back. I hate myself for it."

"We can't do that," Lola interjected. "We can't demonize the past."

Together, the Sheridan women held the silence, tossing their shoes to the side and dropping their feet into the waves. Lola lifted her chest toward the gorgeous sky, feeling the breeze across her skin.

"Tell me again what your itinerary is," Susan finally asked, breaking through the silence.

"Gosh, we're hitting, what, thirteen islands? Fifteen?" Lola began tentatively. "We start on Antigua, which is apparently the largest English-speaking island and offers plenty of historical sites."

"I never thought of Tommy as a history lover," Christine chimed in.

"Gosh, it's ridiculous. He'll watch a seven-hour history documentary rather than do the dishes," Lola said with a laugh.

"The other islands! What are they?" Amanda asked.

"Well..." Lola pushed through her raucous mind. "After Antigua, we sail to Nevis, then St. Kitts, then Saba. That's where we're going to go scuba diving."

"Mom! You didn't tell me you were doing that," Audrey cried.

"That terrifies me," Christine said. "Underwater? For hours at a time? No thanks."

Lola laughed, the sound of it twinkling out across the water. "Then we're going to St. Barts, where they speak French, apparently? Then Anguilla and the British Virgin Islands. Gosh, you look up the images of these, and they're all seafoam green and turquoise and gorgeous twentysomethings on beaches."

"You're a gorgeous woman who will soon be on a beach," Susan countered.

"A honeymoon..." Christine breathed. "I can't imagine that when Zach and I get married, we'll be able to do anything like that."

"Why not?" Audrey and Amanda demanded in unison. "You deserve it."

"Come on. We have a new baby," Christine offered.

The other Sheridan women glanced at one another, perplexed.

"We're there for you, Christine," Audrey finally said. "And by that, we mean, we're there to babysit Mia. You and Zach should run off and celebrate your love, don't you think? You deserve it."

Christine's cheeks burned with a mix of embarrassment and joy. She dropped her gaze toward the water, where seaweed wrapped itself around her ankle. She attempted to kick it off but ultimately failed, laughing as she bent to remove the slimy green strands from her skin.

"I can't tell you how happy I've been lately," Lola breathed, dropping back on the sand, no longer caring what the sand would do to her clothes. "Every day, I come home and think, is this really my life? Is this really my gorgeous husband?"

The rest of the Sheridan women were quiet for a long time, watching the horizon. Lola felt the sand caked into her hair and the back of her head. She imagined herself later, scrubbing herself of sand. It didn't matter. It was summer, wasn't it? That was what summer was for.

* * *

Famous sailor Tommy Gasbarro was seasoned in the art of sailing from Martha's Vineyard to the Caribbean Islands. Three days prior to their departure, he'd written a to-do list that was thirty-five items long, none of which he thought was "that difficult" to figure out. Ultimately, Lola and Tommy found themselves scrambling for the last few items the night before their departure, throwing bread and cheeses and fruits into their grocery cart and laughing at the ridiculous nature of their "getaway." It was now early July, only two days before the Fourth of July, and the island was ridiculously alive, with fireworks blaring in the evening sky, all the way until three in the morning.

They'd decided to depart the docks at seven thirty on the morning of the third, telling everyone that they would sail to the Caribbean, island hop, and return in approximately two weeks. It had been a very long time since Lola felt so free, so alive. And as they prepared the sailboat for departure, she was hardly able to speak. Such was the dramatic nature of her excitement.

Around seven fifteen, when Lola poked her head out of the storage space of the sailboat, she spotted four familiar faces peering out from the far end of the dock. Lola popped up and waved at Audrey, Amanda, Christine, and Susan with her heart in her throat.

"I can't believe they came all the way here to say goodbye," she muttered to Tommy.

"Are you kidding me? Where else would they be?" Tommy shot back.

Lola laughed and leaped from the sailboat, bumbling down the dock toward her daughter, her niece, and her two sisters. She hugged Audrey extra long, obviously, inhaling the density of her brand-new patchouli perfume and asking herself if she was really okay with Audrey moving on from her Ashlee Simpson perfume of yesteryear.

"There he is. Your handsome sailor husband," Christine breathed, drawing an arm over Lola's as they turned back to watch Tommy as he traced a rope around and around his elbow.

"He really is something," Lola affirmed. "But don't tell him that."

"I would never," Christine returned, her grin splitting open.

"You'll send us pictures, won't you?" Audrey asked.

"I don't know," Lola offered. "I had this idea that I could go completely off the grid. Force Tommy to crash into an island. Live out the rest of my days like Tom Hanks in *Cast Away*."

"You think you're really funny, don't you? You're not," Audrey howled.

Lola laughed. "Come on. I'll send you pictures. I'll probably annoy Tommy so much with how much I want to reach out to you."

"Just make sure he doesn't divorce you on the way home," Susan said with a laugh.

"Although if he does, I'll tell him that I have a pretty damn good lawyer," Lola said.

Just before she scampered down the dock to join her new husband, Lola gripped Amanda's hands and glanced down at the ring that now shone prominently. She yanked the hand around to show Susan, both surprised and aghast.

"Did you know about this?" Lola demanded.

"Oh yeah. I just learned when he put the ring on her finger the other day at the Sunrise Cove," Susan said, her laugh erupting over the waters.

"Amanda! When were you planning on telling us?" Lola scolded.

"Come on. She's basically been floating through the air for weeks. If you haven't figured it out by now, you're not paying attention," Audrey said.

"Aud! Are you suggesting that you've known this

whole time and didn't bother to tell me?" Lola demanded.

Audrey shrugged, her smile so crooked that her dimples dug in deep. Lola stepped back, pressing kisses into her palms and blowing them several.

"I'm so grateful for all we have here," she whispered. "And I can't wait to continue summertime with all of you when I get back."

"Get back safe!"

"We love you!"

"Bye!"

Lola felt the words rain down upon her as she scampered back toward Tommy's boat. There, she flung herself into his arms, burrowing her head in his chest as he whispered, "Are you ready?"

Lola had never been more ready for anything in her entire life.

Tommy strung the ropes from the docks, opened the sails, and sped them out across the ocean waves. Lola leaned forward with her chin lifted to allow the salt-filled splashes to course across her cheeks. They were charted down south within a half hour, headed toward the Caribbean. The sun was heavy and bright above them, forcing them to remove their clothing and relax in only swimsuits.

When the waves weren't so frantic, Tommy sat across from Lola in just his swimsuit, his broad chest open and the black hairs of it shining in the sun. Lola placed her feet on either side of his body, lifted her chin, and asked, "So what's next, sailor?"

Tommy laughed, his mouth wide with surprise and joy.

"I guess the rest of our lives," he shot back.

"Good answer." Lola turned to gaze eastward across the horizon with the next spot of land, Europe itself. "If I could have written the story of my life, I couldn't have gotten it quite this good."

Tommy wrapped his hands around her thigh, his thumbs rubbing softly on her sore muscles. Since that wild run on the morning of her wedding, she'd taken to running with exuberance, loving the freedom and the strength. In many ways, she couldn't figure out why she'd never done it before. It seemed to embody everything she adored: streaming through life as fast as you could, with a clear head and a full heart. She prayed she'd live every day with that much enthusiasm. She supposed she had a pretty good chance with Tommy by her side.

Coming Next

Start reading Once in a Lifetime

Other Books by Katie

The Vineyard Sunset Series

Secrets of Mackinac Island Series

Sisters of Edgartown Series

A Katama Bay Series

A Mount Desert Island Series

A Nantucket Sunset Series

Made in the USA
Columbia, SC
12 July 2023

20301874R00108